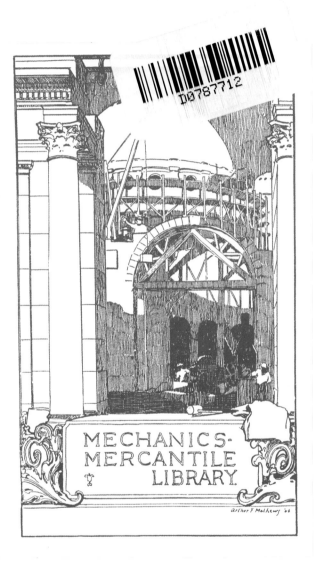

MECHANICS-
MERCANTILE
LIBRARY.

Arthur F Mathews '06

The Stars Above Veracruz

BOOKS BY BARRY GIFFORD

FICTION

The Stars Above Veracruz
Do the Blind Dream?
American Falls: The Collected
Short Stories
Wyoming
My Last Martini
The Sinaloa Story
Baby Cat-Face
Arise and Walk
Night People
Port Tropique

Landscape with Traveler
A Boy's Novel

The Sailor & Lula Novels:
Wild at Heart
Perdita Durango
Sailor's Holiday
Sultans of Africa
Consuelo's Kiss
Bad Day for the Leopard Man

୭

NONFICTION

Read 'Em and Weep: My Favorite Novels
Brando Rides Alone
Out of the Past: Adventures in Film Noir
Las cuatro reinas (with David Perry)
Bordertown (with David Perry)
The Phantom Father: A Memoir
A Day at the Races: The Education of a Racetracker
Saroyan: A Biography (with Lawrence Lee)
The Neighborhood of Baseball
Jack's Book: An Oral Biography of Jack Kerouac (with Lawrence Lee)

The Stars Above Veracruz

∽∽∽∽∽∽∽∽∽∽∽∽

Barry Gifford

THUNDER'S MOUTH PRESS
NEW YORK

The Stars Above Veracruz

Thunder's Mouth Press
An Imprint of Avalon Publishing Group Inc.
245 West 17th Street • 11th Floor
New York, NY 10011

AVALON
publishing group incorporated

"The Law of Affection" and "One Leg" appeared in *Confabulario,* the cultural supplement of *El Universal* (Mexico City). "After Hours at La
Chinita" appeared in the anthology *San Francisco Noir* (New York). The
following publications provided source material for "Murder at the
Swordfish Club": *Tales of the Angler's Eldorado* by Zane Grey (Grosset &
Dunlap, 1926); *Bay of Islands Swordfish Club Yearbook Diamond Jubilee Edition
1924-1984; New Zealand* edited by Gordon Mclauchlan (APA Produc-
tions, 1986); *New Zealand Handbook* by Jane King (Moon Publications,
1987); *New Zealand: A Travel Survival Kit* by Tony Wheeler (Lonely Planet,
1985); and *Tides of History: Bay of Islands County* by Kay Boese (Bay of
Islands County Council, 1977). The author wishes to thank the directors
of the Bay of Islands Swordfish Club in Russell, New Zealand, for
allowing him access to the club archives; and special thanks to Ross Davey,
for his assistance. "The Stars Above Veracruz" appeared in the magazine
Dazed and Confused (London); *Confabulario* (Mexico City); and the *San
Francisco Chronicle* Sunday Magazine.

Library of Congress Cataloging-in-Publication Data is available.

ISBN: 1-56025-807-1
ISBN 13: 978-1-56025-807-0

9 8 7 6 5 4 3 2 1

Book design by Susan Canavan
Printed in the United States of America
Distributed by Publishers Group West

Contents

To Commander L. E. Colby, ret.

The past is a foreign country. They do things
differently there.

—L. P. Hartley,
The Go-Between

The Ropedancer:
An Introduction

ഗഗഗഗഗഗഗഗഗഗ

Veracruz

I AM A FUNAMBULIST. I WAS TRAINED AS A ROPEWALKER, or ropedancer, from my third birthday, and I performed with my parents, the Dancing Ciegas, until they plunged to their deaths from a high wire when I was sixteen years old. Following this tragedy, I made a decision to stop performing. That was forty years ago.

My parents, Celso Ugalde and Celia Matos, took as their professional name Ciega, blind in Spanish, because they performed blindfolded, most often without a net. The net was used only when I appeared with them, and then only until I was twelve years old. I was tall for my age and my father decided, over the objection of my mother, that twelve was the proper age for me to assume responsibility for the integrity of the act. I was eager to do so and did my best to convince my mother that I had no fear of "walking naked," as it was described by the fraternity of acrobats and wire artists.

Until that fateful day when I became an orphan, all went well as we toured throughout Mexico and Guatemala with the Circo Garibaldi. Nobody named Garibaldi was involved with the circus, but it was presumed by the owner, a skinny juggler named Orfeo Fideo, that an Italian pedigree would be deemed by potential customers as both more exotic and authentic than one of Spanish or Indian origin. I was billed on the program as *Il Funàmbolo Piccolissimo* to lend an even greater exotic air to the act.

My funambulism for the past forty years has been, therefore, of a figurative, even metaphorical nature, a demonstration consisting solely of mental agility. I became an observer and eventually a recorder of events, evidence of which defines as a funambulist each of us who dares to take a step.

At sixteen, I went to live in the Hotel Los Regalos de los Dios in the port city of Veracruz, a place I had always liked because of its feeling of impermanence, the ships coming and going and the buildings crumbling all around, decaying from the salt air. Though I have traveled some, I have ever since maintained my residence in the Regalos de Dios, which is located on Calle Las Pesadillas de los Santos, next to the railyards where I continue to work as a boxcar cleaner. I have never married.

Recently, a resident of the hotel hanged himself in his room. He was a cripple, a man with only one leg. It was the night clerk, Paco Fatigado, who discovered the corpse and cut him down. Later, Paco told me this man's story. He had been in love with his own sister, who was much younger than he, more than ten years. They had become lovers when she was fourteen or fifteen. She married when she was twenty-two, which made her brother crazy, and he left Mexico for several years. When he returned, he went to see his sister. She refused his advances, so he raped her. She became pregnant and had her brother's child, a boy, but he was deformed, a hunchback, and demented. The sister confessed to her husband that her brother had been her lover and had fathered this unfortunate child by force.

Her husband attempted to murder her brother with a knife, succeeding only in severing a major artery in his brother-in-law's leg, which necessitated its amputation. The husband, however, was stabbed to death by the brother with his own knife. This incident, combined with the fact that his sister vowed never to see or talk to him again, a vow she kept, drove the man into the depths of a sadness from which he could not recover, a calamitous circumstance that ended, for him, in the Hotel Los Regalos de los Dios when he lost his balance forever. Even had he the use of both legs, they would not have saved him. Instead of walking across the rope he finished by dancing at the end of it.

I know many stories such as this, equally tragic, devastating portraits of damaged souls and wasted lives. I've always been a good listener, and the Hotel Los Regalos de los Dios, being something of a repository for lost travelers who often find themselves in a confessional mode, has proven to be a treasure trove of tales, mostly of woe. Those that follow are among the most interesting I have heard, remembered and written down.

Rodolfo Fierro

"El Carcinero"

once shot a stranger

in Ciudad Chihuahua

to settle a bet

as to

whether a dying man

would fall

forward

or backward

Fierro predicted the

man

would

fall forward

he won

the bet

The Law of Affection
 споспоспоспоспоспоспоспоспоспоспоспоспоспоспоспоспо
Honduras

MY UNCLE BUCK HAD BIG PLANS FOR HIS INVESTMENT IN
Honduras. In the early 1970s, he bought a piece of property on the island of Utila, in the Bay Islands, off the coast
across from La Ceiba. He owned fifteen hundred feet of
beachfront and envisioned a vacation paradise that
included gambling—which was legal in Honduras—
luxury hotels, sailing, speedboats, etc. Buck, who was a
civil engineer, built himself an octagonal house on stilts;
when the tide came in it was necessary to use a boat to
get to dry land. For this purpose, Uncle Buck kept a
dinghy with a small outboard motor tied to one of the
stilts next to a ladder. A person could easily swim to

shore, he told me, but the bay was shark-infested, which rendered that option a bit risky.

My uncle claimed the island was governed by witchcraft, or voodoo, but in reality the few hundred inhabitants, who were mostly descendants of pirates, slave traders and slaves, and who bore surnames such as Morgan, Jones, and Lafitte, were motivated and inspired more by superstition than anything else. The people were very poor, and, my uncle's grandiose ideas notwithstanding, there was virtually no tourism during the twenty years he lived there.

There was, however, soon after Uncle Buck sold his property on Utila, a terrible hurricane that devastated much of the Bay Islands, as well as Tegucigalpa, the capital of the country. My uncle had a good life there for a while. He was about sixty when he moved to Utila, and he soon acquired Juana, who was then sixteen, as his island girl. My uncle spoke fluent Spanish and taught Juana English. She took care of the property when Buck was away, and, years later, when Juana wanted to immigrate to the United States, he helped her gain residency in Tampa, Florida, where he also kept a home. Juana eventually married a man in Tampa and she and my uncle remained good friends until the end of his life. In fact, she was at his bedside in the hospital when he died, two weeks before what would have been his ninety-third birthday.

One time when I was with Uncle Buck in Tampa, he told me that Bobby Robinson, a friend of his on the island, had been arrested for shooting to death a mutual acquaintance of theirs named George Morgan. Robinson and Morgan had been at a picnic with their families and friends when a dispute arose over a card game. Apparently, the two men, who were both in their late twenties, and who had known each other all of their lives, had argued heatedly for a short time, then stopped. The others present thought it was finished, but an hour or so later Bobby, who may have been drunk, took a pistol and fired a bullet into George Morgan's left temple, killing him instantly.

My uncle received a letter a couple of weeks after this incident occurred from another friend on the island, Spurgeon Bush, who owned the only appliance store there. Bush, who had been at the picnic, told Buck what happened and that Bobby Robinson was being held in the island jail. Uncle Buck placed a call to his friend Prince Albert, the sheriff, at the jail, and Bobby Robinson answered the telephone.

"Bobby, what are you doing answering the phone?" asked my uncle. "I thought you were being held on a murder charge."

"I'm playing checkers with Prince Albert," Bobby said, "at his desk, so when it rang I just picked it up."

"Did you shoot Morgan?" Buck asked.

"Yes," said Bobby, "but it was an accident. Prince Albert says he's going to release me as soon as the investigation has been completed."

"Let me talk to Albert," said my uncle. "*Buena suerte,* Bobby."

"*Gracias, Señor Buck. Hasta pronto.*"

Bobby passed the receiver to Prince Albert and Buck asked him for the details.

"Bobby didn't mean to shoot George Morgan," the sheriff told my uncle. "And nobody minds that Morgan is dead. He was an unpopular fellow, as you know."

"Were there any witnesses?" asked Buck.

"Very many witnesses," said Prince Albert. "I have collected many statements already. Everyone says Bobby did not mean to kill Morgan. It was an old gun with a faulty firing pin. Bobby didn't think it would go off."

"But it did," said Buck.

"For better or worse, yes," replied the sheriff.

"What about Morgan's family? He had a wife and a child, didn't he? Who's going to take care of them?"

"Morgan's wife, Victoria, is Bobby's first cousin," said Prince Albert. "He says she will be all right with his family. Victoria was not happy with Morgan. She will find another man. Maybe me. Victoria is very pretty still, you remember."

"I don't think I know her," said Buck.

"You will. When you return to the island, we will invite you to my house for supper."

A couple of years later, in my uncle's house, I met Spurgeon Bush, the appliance store proprietor. We were sitting in the guest bedroom. Spurgeon always called me *sobrino,* nephew in Spanish. He showed me a silver-plated .38 he said he always carried, and a business card on which was printed a telephone number and the name of a general in the Honduran army.

"Turn over the card," Spurgeon said. "Read the words written above the signature."

"Este hombre esta bajo mi protección."

"These are the six most important words to possess in my country. This is my *permiso.*"

"Your permission for what?" I asked him.

"To kill," said Spurgeon. "I am a special agent under the authority of the general. Nobody will harm me."

"What about the appliance business?"

"What about it?"

"If I angered you by buying a refrigerator from another store, you could shoot me and not be charged with murder."

Spurgeon Bush smiled, revealing several gold teeth. "You forget, *sobrino,* I am the only refrigerator dealer on Utila."

I handed him back his *permiso.*

"Unlike others in Honduras," Spurgeon said, "I use my gun only for the most high reasons."

"What about Bobby Robinson?" I asked. "Did he have a good reason to shoot George Morgan?"

"The best," said Spurgeon Bush. "Victoria, Morgan's wife, was Bobby's first cousin, but they had been lovers since they were children. The child was Bobby's, not Morgan's."

"Morgan knew this?"

Spurgeon shrugged his shoulders.

"Did Bobby have a *permiso,* also?" I asked.

"No, otherwise Prince Albert would not have been able to arrest him. But Bobby had the right."

"I would think, as Victoria's husband," I said, "that George Morgan, if he knew the child was not his, would have had the right to kill Bobby."

Spurgeon stood up and tucked the silver-plated .38 into his waistband. He was wearing powder-blue belt-less slacks and a jungle-green guayabera. Spurgeon was not particularly tall but he was stocky with hands like meat cleavers. His skin was what they called on the island *pardo,* mud brown, and his face was riddled with pockmarks. He had a deep scar on his nose, shaped like an anchor.

Spurgeon Bush smiled at me again and laid a meat cleaver on one of my shoulders.

"Sobrino," he said, "nobody liked George Morgan."

Now there's a man
            know how to do
        some serious damage
            to a woman
                whether she got
                    black stripes
                    down her back
                    or not

After Hours at La Chinita

〜〜〜〜〜〜〜〜〜〜〜

Los Angeles

IT WAS LATE AT NIGHT IN A MOTEL OFFICE. THE FURNISHINGS were shabby. La Chinita, once an elegant, Spanish-style motel built in the 1930s, was now, in 1963, run-down; paint was peeling off the walls and the wooden registration desk was chipped and gouged. An old, moth-eaten easy chair and a few other rickety wickers with ripped seats and backs were placed against the walls. Hanging blinds, with several slats missing or broken, covered the glass-paned door. The office was clean, however, and presided over by a bespectacled woman who looked to be in her mid-sixties. She was seated in a lounge chair in front of the desk, knitting and humming softly to herself. Her name was Vermillion Chaney. The tune she was humming was "Just a Closer Walk with Thee." It was two weeks before Christmas.

The telephone behind the motel desk rang. Vermillion did not move. The telephone continued to ring. It was as if Vermillion did not hear it. The telephone rang eight times before it finally stopped. After the telephone stopped ringing, Vermillion put down her knitting, stood up and walked behind the registration desk, picked up the telephone receiver and dialed a number.

"Was that you just called?" Vermillion asked into the phone. "Um, okay. Don't matter. What you doin', anyway? Sure I know it's three o'clock in the mornin', I'm at work!"

Vermillion hung up the phone. She came back around the desk, sat back down in her chair and resumed knitting. She started singing again, only this time the tune was "What a Friend We Have in Jesus."

The office door began to shake. Somebody was trying to open it but the door was locked. This was followed by loud knocking. The knocking was hard, insistent.

From behind the door came a woman's scream. "Open up! Open the door!"

Vermillion stopped singing and stared at the door. The knocking continued. The woman's voice became hysterical.

"You got to help me! Open up!"

Vermillion put down her knitting, got up and went to the door. She looked out through one of the missing slats as the woman outside continued to yell.

"Miz Chaney, it's me! Revancha!"

Vermillion unlocked the door and a woman in her early twenties burst into the office, forcing the older woman back as she brushed past her.

"Shut it!" said Revancha. "Lock that door before he gets here!"

Vermillion stared at the young woman, who was wearing only a bra and panties. Clutched to her chest were other garments. Vermillion closed the door. Revancha ran back to it and fastened the chain lock.

"What's goin' on, Revancha? You look like a chicken in a bag full of snakes."

Revancha retreated from the door and stopped with her back against the desk.

"He beatin' on me, Miz Chaney! Chokin' me! Usin' a strap!"

"Man get what he pay for."

"He gone too far, cat flip his wig! Call security!"

Vermillion walked back behind the desk, reached down and came up with a revolver in her right hand.

"This the onliest security I got tonight, baby."

"Where's Myron?" asked Revancha.

Vermillion shook her head.

"He out the loop. Fool got hisself arrested yestiday for receivin' stolen property. Fake beaver coats. Can you beat that? I'm alone here this evenin'."

The office door started to shake.

A man shouted, "Vermillion! Let me in!" He rattled the door.

"Don't do it, Miz Chaney!" said Revancha.

"Bitch stole my pants!"

"You'd best go on, Ray," said Vermillion.

"Not without my pants!"

Vermillion looked at Revancha.

"You got Ray's pants?"

"I scooped it all up, what was piled on the floor. Thought maybe he wouldn't follow me."

"Man ain't gonna go away without you give up his trousers."

Ray forced himself against the door, breaking the lock on the handle. Only the chain now prevented him from opening the door. He stuck his hand through the opening and attempted to undo the chain.

"Don't do it, Ray," said Vermillion, "I got a piece."

Ray pushed against the door, breaking the chain. The door flew open and Ray entered. He was a handsome man in his mid-thirties, wearing only a white dress shirt, half-unbuttoned, undershorts, socks and shoes. He moved toward Revancha.

"Give me my wallet," he said.

Vermillion pointed the gun at him.

"Stop right there, Ray," she said. "I'll get it for you."

Ray stopped.

"I ain't got your wallet!" shrieked Revancha.

Ray brushed past Vermillion and grabbed the garments Revancha was holding out of her hands. He felt around in them.

"It ain't here!"

He dropped the garments on the floor and grabbed hold of Revancha.

"Where is it?!"

"Let go the girl, Ray!" said Vermillion.

Ray put his hands around Revancha's throat and began choking her. Revancha screamed; she kept screaming.

"Turn her loose, Ray, or I got to shoot!"

Ray turned his head and looked at Vermillion but continued strangling the girl.

"You old whore," Ray said to Vermillion, "you prob'ly in on the game."

Vermillion trained the barrel of her revolver on Ray and pulled the trigger, shooting him in the side. Ray, stunned, looked down at himself and watched as blood began to stain his shirt. Revancha continued to scream. Ray looked back at the girl and tightened his grip around her throat. Vermillion fired again, this time hitting Ray square in the back. His hands came away from Revancha's throat. He turned slowly and faced the old lady. She fired a third bullet, which entered his body in the middle of his chest. Ray dropped to his knees, holding his hands up, as if in prayer. He remained motionless in that position for several moments before toppling over onto his face.

Revancha stopped screaming. She looked down at Ray. Blood was everywhere.

From behind them came a man's voice: "Mother of God."

Vermillion turned and saw a short, middle-aged, long-bearded man, dressed like a tramp, standing in the doorway. The tramp took a closer look at Ray's corpse, crossed himself and said, "If God knew what He was doing, He wouldn't be doing this."

಄

A nightclub. The stage was dark. A single spotlight came on, shining on an empty stool set in the middle of the stage. A microphone lay on the stool.

The voice of the club announcer boomed out at the audience.

"And now, ladies and gentlemen, the moment you have all been waiting for. The Top Hat, New York's premier supper club, is proud to welcome America's favorite recording artist, direct from the Coast, Mr. Smooth himself, Ray Sparks!"

As the audience applauded, Ray Sparks, the man who was gunned down in the motel office, skipped onstage. He was nattily dressed in a sharp suit and tie.

Lights came up behind him, revealing an orchestra, which began to play. Ray smiled and bowed to the audience, who continued to applaud. He then turned and picked up the microphone, sat down on the stool and began to sing.

ꙮ

Twenty years later. In the corridor of a decrepit nursing home, elderly people, mostly black, were either sitting in or being pushed along in wheelchairs by attendants. One of the former, a woman in her eighties, sat in a wheelchair placed flush against a wall, ignored by the overworked staff. The woman, now blind, wearing dark glasses, was Vermillion Chaney.

"I don't recall that night too good," said Vermillion. "I'm old enough now I don't recall most too good, though sometimes I surprise myself, rememberin' the tiniest detail from way back in the day. I knowed Revancha was a workin' girl, sure I did. Used to be she hung out at the Toro Club down Figueroa. Almost always she'd bring her man to the Chinita. Never had no trouble about her until that night.

"Ray Sparks? Everybody knowed Ray Sparks. Famous singer like him? Nobody miss that face. I heard he sometimes hung at the Toro, sat in with the band, after hours, like that. Maybe he just run into Revancha for the first time. Can't say one way or another. About the shootin', it's like I told the po-lice when it happen, I was just defendin' the girl and myself."

∾

Revancha Lopez, now in her mid-forties, was seated on a bed in a crummy hotel room. The evidence of a hard life showed in her face.

"My name is Esquerita Revancha Lopez y Arrieta. I ain't been usin' for six years, since before my last holiday at Tehachapi, and I won't start again, the Good Lord willin'. The street broke me. If you can believe this, I got me a straight job now, cleanin' rooms at the Chinita. Ain't that a twist? 'Bout that night, I heard so many stories, 'bout the man bein' set up and all, 'bout Miz Chaney be in on a hustle, even that she and I was hired by the FBI or a black militant group to put him out the way. People make up shit like that don't need no TV. They got enough goin' on inside they own mind entertain theyself.

"I knew Ray Sparks for a while before that. He had this image, you know, clean livin' man, good family, still singin' gospel some Sundays. Cat was a player! Not only that but I heard his wife was runnin' the streets, too. I had just got back to the Toro Club after doin' a piece of business when in walk Ray with his cousin, Anthony. Was Anthony come over to me, buy me a drink. We shootin' the shit for a few moments, then here come Ray. Puts his arm around me, says somethin' like, 'Señorita Lopez, I figure it's about time you treat me right.' I said, 'You got what it takes, Ray.' We was playin', straight up. He'd had a few drinks already, he didn't want no more, and he was all over *me,* tellin' me how beautiful I look, he don't know why we ain't got together before, makin' me feel good. Back then, it don't take but fifty dollars to make me feel good, but Ray, he liked to have some style, you know what I'm sayin'? He know it's gonna cost him, but he liked to play like it's on the house. One thing, with this girl was nothin' doin' on the house.

"Now I'd been with Anthony before, so Ray, he know the deal. The three of us was havin' a good time.

Ray be rubbin' against me, I knew he was ready to do some business. Inside an hour, we get in his red Corvette, tool over to the Chinita. I ask him, 'Don't you want to do better than this?' He say, 'Baby, I'm in a hurry to get at you.' Okay by me. I didn't figure him to be a freak. I ask for a hundred dollars. Star like him can't think under that. He pay for the privilege of bein' a star. He took off his pants. I got down to my underwear and next thing I know, he starts beatin' on me. I mean, *serious,* usin' a belt. I tell him to quit, he don't need to be doin' that. He say, 'Don't tell me what I need!' He throw me down on the bed, push my face into a pillow so I can't scream, hittin' me. Then he sticks his dick in from behind, finish in a hurry. Then he get up, go into the bathroom.

"When I hear him relievin' himself, I jump up, scoop all the clothes off the floor and run out the room. I run to the office. Miz Chaney let me in, she by herself, lock the door. A few seconds later, Ray bust it down. Miz Chaney be afraid for her life, that's the truth. He come at me, shoutin' I stolen his wallet. Chokin' me. Miz Chaney come up with a hand cannon, tell Ray turn me loose. Next thing I know, there's Ray on the floor, everywhere is red. It weren't the worst time in my life, but it was sure the beginnin' of a downhill. I keep thinkin', slide got to stop sometime. I keep thinkin', but it don't really stop."

∾

Ray Sparks was half-seated on a nightclub stool.

"Who you're lookin' at ain't Ray Sparks, it's the ghost of Ray Sparks. Here it is twenty years later, and I look the same, not like Revancha Lopez and Vermillion Chaney. You'll have to decide for yourself if it's a comfort to look like you did when you died on into eternity. They don't look so good as me but they got to live a lot longer. What people do with their lives is mostly fuck 'em up. Almost no way they could do anything else. I always liked that saying, give a man enough rope and he'll hang himself. Just some folks got themselves a longer rope, is all. And Malcolm, he told me Josef Stalin said, 'A capitalist will sell you the rope to hang him with.'

"People like to blame other people for their own troubles. Even me. One thing I picked up on recently— in eternity, all thoughts and things are recent—is how there is no particular way to avoid what you do or how you do it. It's like wakin' up in the middle of the night, hung over, and snorin' in the bed next to you is an ugly whore. And you think to yourself, this can't be me, shacked up with some nasty skank. Me is little Ray, runnin' with my dog down along the river. Seven years old, me and my dog runnin' next to the river and it's about to rain. Nobody botherin' us. But no mistake, it's you in that bed, feelin' like a bomb gone off in your head, and that ain't no cute puppy lyin' there. You got to ask yourself why, and then if you got a lick of sense, do somethin' to change your situation. If you never ask yourself the question, Why?, then you ain't got a chance. You got to be brave. Ray Sparks never gave himself the opportunity to be brave."

"Don't you be listenin' to that man!" said Vermillion Chaney, who rolled herself up to Ray in her wheelchair. "Talk like he sang, smooth as silk.

"Didn't shoot you on purpose," she said.

"What you mean, didn't do it on purpose?" said Ray. "That was on purpose as possible to be. You shot me three times, once in the back."

"Pistol felt light as a feather in my hand."

"You got to like pullin' that trigger."

"Light as a feather," said Vermillion.

Revancha walked up to Ray and said, "I didn't mean to steal your clothes."

"Only my wallet."

"Your wallet was up in those clothes somewhere. I would have left it, after I took what was owed me."

"There's no such thing as an honest whore," said Ray.

"Man get violent, what's a woman to do?" said Vermillion. "God put that gun in my hand, told me to use it."

"Better to leave God out of this," said Ray.

"When I was a little girl, eight years old," said Revancha, "Mamacita took me down on Calle Olvera to La Iglesia Espiritu Santu, to pray for my father, who was in the prison hospital. He had got stabbed in the stomach in a fight. We didn't know it then, but at that same moment we was in the church, he died. I liked lightin' the candles.

"We was about to leave when a man come in off the street, wearin' nothin' but dirty rags. Had a long beard. I said, 'Mama, look, it's Jesus Cristo!' The man started blowin' out all the candles, then picked 'em up and stuffed as many as he could inside his shirt. He looked up at the cross and shook his fist at it. He shouted,

'There's no hiding place for the damned!' Then he ran out of the church, droppin' candles as he went.

"When Mama and I got home, we found out my father was dead. I asked Mamacita, 'Is Papa damned?' *'No se,'* she said, 'I don't know.' "

"I heard that after I died," said Ray, "there was a church created in my name. The Church of Ray Sparks."

"You coulda been a saint, Ray," said Vermillion, "but instead you was a fool."

"I'd like to've gone to the Church of Ray Sparks, shown up without nobody knowin' I was comin'. Got up in front of the choir and sung, 'He's My Friend Until the End.' "

"There ain't no such church," said Revancha.

"Heard there was."

"The devil got your ear, son," said Vermillion, "way he go about flatterin' folks. He do that. Vain man fallin' for the devil's malarkey, that all that is."

"What you had to go smackin' me around like that for, anyway?" asked Revancha. "Use me so bad."

"Standin' in Satan's shoes," said Vermillion, "even back then."

"Man spoke the truth," said Ray.

"What man?" asked Revancha.

"One you saw in your church, stole all the candles. No place to hide."

"John the Baptis'," said Vermillion.

"I know him, I know that man."

"How could you?" said Revancha.

"Look at him, sugar, a child of darkness. All the devil's children the same. Ask him can he sing, Revancha. Go on."

"Can you sing, Ray?"

" 'Course I can sing."

"Tell him go ahead and try," said Vermillion.

"Sing, Ray. Sing, 'He's My Friend Until the End.' "

Ray opened his mouth to sing but no sound came out. He tried again with the same result.

"I can't."

"The Lord giveth and the Lord taketh away," said Vermillion. "You ain't got no gift left, Mister Church of Ray Sparks."

Ray got up and walked away.

"Damn, Miz Chaney," said Revancha, "that's hard."

"He ask for it."

Revancha began to cry.

"Only times I ever have an orgasm," she said, "is when I imagine the man doin' me the one dressed in rags come in the church day my father died."

"God bless you, girl," said Vermillion.

"God bless you, too, Miz Chaney."

That road broke

my heart

too much

times

already

man

you goin'

without

me

What Happened in Japan

∽∽∽∽∽∽∽∽∽∽∽

France

BOBBY NEWBY HAD BEEN STUCK FOR MORE THAN AN hour in a rainstorm in the little town of Ligny-en-poisson. He was hitchhiking from Strasbourg to Paris, his last ride having been with a priest who spoke no English. Since Bobby did not speak French, they had ridden in silence from Nancy to Ligny, where the priest dropped Bobby before turning off the main road, headed to some other village.

Bobby, who was eighteen years old, was traveling alone in Europe; meandering, really, touring on the cheap by thumb and the occasional train. It was a Sunday and he walked through the shuttered-up streets looking for a café in which to have some coffee or tea and get out of the weather. Nothing was open; the entire town was asleep. Finally, as he was approaching a little bridge over a swollen stream at the edge of town, he heard the whir of a small engine. He turned and stuck out his thumb. A tiny Renault skidded to a halt in front of him. Bobby opened the door on the passenger side and a stack of boxes cascaded onto the road.

"Just throw them into the backseat and get in!" shouted the driver.

Once Bobby was settled into the seat, with boxes behind, below, to the sides and on top of him, the driver, who was a man of about thirty, explained that they were full of girdles and other undergarments, samples from the factory in Paris, where he was headed. Bobby told him that was where he was going and the man said he would take him there.

"I'm a salesman," said the man. "My name is François Ruisselet."

"Bobby Newby. You speak English."

"And some Japanese, too. Where are you from, Bobby? America or Canada?"

"St. Louis. How could you tell?"

"By your clothes. Ah, *la rivière Mississippi*. I would love to see it. Is the water blue or green?"

"Brown, mostly. It's muddy and dirty."

"When I was a boy, I read about Huckleberry Finn and his *compère, le négrillon,* Jim. How I would like to have been on their raft with them! What an adventure. But I have adventures, too. You see, I meet these young girls in the towns I visit, in the cafés and bars, and they are unsophisticated, innocent. I tell them about Paris, the fabulous lights, the Seine, the restaurants, the night-clubs they've never seen except in movies. I tell them I work for a famous manufacturer. A manufacturer of what? they ask. Lingerie, I say, *porte-jarretelles.* Ones designed especially for movie stars and dancers. All of the best-known actresses wear our foundations. *Vraiment?* they say. Really? *Bien sûr, naturellement,* I tell them."

François swerved his Renault to avoid hitting a black dog that was sniffing at the inert body of a small animal lying in the road. The dog did not move as they rushed past it.

"I take the girl out to the car," François said, "move the boxes from the backseat to the front and get into the back with the girl. *Regard!* I say, and I remove from one of the boxes a flimsy pair of silk panties. Feel this, I tell her, and she runs the tips of her fingers over the silk and lace. *Oo-la-la,* she squeals, *c'est magnifique.* She's never felt such soft, exquisite material before. I ask her if she'd like to try them on. She turns red, she giggles. Go on, I urge her, nobody can see you here in the car. And, of course, she does. As soon as she takes off her own underwear, I've got her, she's mine."

"Do you give her the panties to keep?" Bobby asked.

"Of course not, I couldn't do that," said François. "I would have to pay for them. I tell her that I will send her a box of the best as soon as I get to Paris, but I never do. I mean, that would be crazy. I'll never see this girl again, and besides, our lingerie is too expensive."

They were already in Paris when François told Bobby, "Once I went to Tokyo for the company, in 1962, two years ago. It's the only time I've been beyond Europe. I almost didn't come back because of a girl I met there. These French girls haven't got a clue about what it takes to please a man."

François pulled the Renault to the curb and left the motor running. It was still raining, but not so hard.

"This is Pont Neuf," he said. "We are in the center

of Paris. If I had more time, I would tell you what happened in Japan, but I'm already late. My wife will be angry with me as it is. *Bonne chance.*"

"Thanks for the ride," said Bobby.

He got out of the car, making sure none of the boxes tumbled into the street, and closed the door. François waved quickly at him and sped off into the traffic. Bobby looked around, then began to walk across the bridge. He thought about Japan.

In Mexico some people

believe birds work

for the devil

they fly around

and identify

for Satan the weak

and wicked

whom he comes for later

to my knowledge

there are no birds

in hell

Almost Oriental

Romania

FOR Andrei Codrescu

Prelude

A winter's day in Chicago, 1951. Snow coated the ground. Solomon Traum, eighty-one years old, with dark hair and a bushy mustache, was standing on the street in front of an elevated station, smoking a cigar. Despite the icy wind, he wore only a woollen sport coat with a muffler wrapped around his neck. A powder-blue Cadillac pulled up, driven by his forty-one-year-old-son, Rudolph "Buddy" Traum. The passenger door was on the curb side. The old man walked to the car. Buddy reached over and opened the door. Solomon slowly climbed in and closed it.

"Pa, for Chrissakes," said Buddy, "why don't you wear an overcoat? It's cold."

The old man did not look over or answer right away. Buddy began to drive.

"What cold?" said the old man. "In the *old* country was cold."

1.

LEAVES FLUTTERED FROM THE TREES AS STUDENTS AND faculty members walked across the Stanford University campus. Robert Botto, thirty-eight, a professor of American Literature, was greeted by and returned the greetings of others, as he made his way toward his office. He entered a building and went up the stairs. The telephone in his office began ringing just as he opened the door. He sat down behind his desk and picked up the receiver.

"Robert Botto.

"Oh, hello, Sally.

"Well, you knew it snowed a lot in Denver before you moved there.

"Yes, I'll send the check for Rebecca before I leave.

"The twenty-third.

"I'm glad she and Edward are getting along so well."

There was a knock on the door, which Robert had not bothered to close completely. He looked up and saw a young man, a student of his. Robert motioned for him to come in and sit down in the chair on the other side of Robert's desk. The student entered, closed the door and sat down.

"Yes, Sally, I'm still here.

"Look, I know we have to talk about these things, but right now I'm in a bit of a rush.

"A couple of weeks, maybe more.

"Of course I want to see her.

"After that, then.

"When does her school start?

"No, I don't expect Edward to pay for it. We'll work it out. Listen, I have someone here right now.

"All right, yes. Bye."

He hung up the receiver, took a moment to look out the window to recover his composure, then turned to his visitor.

"Hi, Matt."

"I didn't mean to interrupt."

"Conversations with ex-wives often require interruption."

"When do you leave?"

"Tomorrow."

"Romania?"

"Austria first, Vienna. Then Romania."

"Traum grew up in Vienna, didn't he?"

"He spent a few years there, as a boy, but I think he was born in a region called the Bucovina, which until the end of World War I belonged to Austria. He came with his family to America after the war."

"The only thing of his I've read is a novel, *The Enchanted*."

Robert got up, went to his bookshelf, took down a book and handed it to Matt.

"This is his memoir, *The Phantom Father*. You can read it while I'm gone."

Matt stood up and accepted the book.

"Why is it called *The Phantom Father*?"

"Because Buddy didn't know him very well. He died when Buddy was twelve."

"The past is always a mystery, isn't it?"

Robert went to the door and opened it.

"The past is not dead," said Robert, "it's not even past."

Matt walked to the door and stopped.

"That's pretty good," he said.

"William Faulkner said it in his Nobel Prize speech."

"When will you be back?"

Robert smiled. "Who knows? I may never be back."

"I get to keep the book then, right?"

"Keep it anyway."

"Have a good trip, professor."

Matt went out. Robert closed the door.

2.

VINCENZU DUDA, EIGHTY-TWO YEARS OLD, WAS SEATED in a wheelchair. Robert wheeled him into the nursing home solarium, where he stopped and sat down in a chair next to Duda's.

"Did you know that my father's family came from the Bucovina, too?" asked Vincenzu Duda.

"I didn't."

"I didn't know it myself until three or four years ago, just after Buddy came back from Vienna. I always thought my people had come from Russia, they spoke Russian, but my sister set me straight. Buddy and I knew each other for almost seventy years, since we were kids in Chicago, and it wasn't until the last couple that we knew our families came from the same place. We talked about going there together, but then Buddy died and I got hit by lightning again."

"Again?" said Robert, a half-amused, half-pained expression on his face.

"Sixth or seventh time, I lost count. Something in my system attracts the sparks, I guess. Doctors never have been able to figure it out. Told me I should have an indoors job. Lightning bolt would probably come down the chimney to find me. Almost did, once. Traveled down a rain gutter where I was working, diggin' a trench.

"Why do you think Buddy made all those references to lightning in his books? Ball lightning, ribbon lightning, bead lightning, they all come after me. Buddy got all his information about it from me, first hand. Most people get struck by lightning on open water, you know that?"

"So I've heard."

"I wasn't just Buddy's oldest friend, I was one of his characters. You've read his books, haven't you?"

"I have."

"Okay, then."

Duda began coughing, a fit that lasted for almost a minute.

"Too bad I can't go with you," he went on, "but this last strike just about buried me. My heart stopped beating for two minutes, the medics said. Not only that, but all those years as a plumber tore my knees up inside.

"About the best I can hope for now is an accommodating nurse. You know, a blow job and a shot of morphine now and then."

Robert laughed, and said, "I'm leaving tomorrow for Vienna, Mr. Duda. I'll stay there for a few days and then move on to the Bucovina. I'll try to get some information about your family, too."

"Call me Vincenzu, not Vincenzo, that's Italian. My mother was Italian. Italian-American, anyway. My father named me. Vincenzu was his grandfather's name. But you're here about Buddy. He used the name 'Rudolph' on his books, you know."

"Yes."

"I told him he should use Buddy, that's what everybody called him, even at school."

"I know from his diaries that at one point he considered using the name 'Reveur' instead of Traum."

" 'Reveur' is French, isn't it?"

" 'Traum' is 'dream' in German. Reveur means 'dreamer' in French."

"You know a lot."

"If I'm going to write his biography, I have to know all I can."

"Or die tryin'."

A large male nurse entered the solarium.

"Time for your nap, Mr. Duda," said the nurse.

Vincenzu looked at the nurse, then at Robert.

"Story of my life."

As the male nurse began to wheel Vincenzu away, the old man shouted back to Robert, "Remember, no open water."

"I'll remember," said Robert.

3.

ROBERT WAS IN THE BEDROOM OF HIS APARTMENT, packing, an open suitcase on the bed. As he filled the suitcase, he looked at a picture of his daughter in a frame on his dresser. He picked it up and stared at it. He began to put it into his suitcase, then decided against taking it and replaced it on the dresser. He continued packing.

4.

Robert, wearing a heavy overcoat, scarf and a hat to protect him from the fast-falling snow, walked up the steps of the Hall of Records in Vienna and entered the building.

Inside the hall, Robert stopped at an information desk and showed his identification to the woman staffing it. People passed briskly in and out of the building as she copied his passport number onto a piece of paper. She handed Robert's passport back to him and pointed toward an elevator. Robert nodded to her and proceeded in the direction in which she pointed.

Robert was seated at a small desk in the archive room, surrounded by shelves of books and filing cabinets, examining a stack of papers. The archive clerk approached him and set another pile of folders, papers and reference books on the desk in front of Robert.

"I'm afraid we have no information about Solomon

Traum after the year 1918," the clerk told him. "According to the city directory from 1917, he was a resident at number five Zirkusgasse in Leopoldstadt, which was a Jewish district in Vienna."

"What about the birth certificates for the children?" asked Robert.

"There is nothing. The only document we have is this."

The clerk handed a piece of paper to Robert, who examined it closely.

The clerk continued: "This is a copy of an exit visa issued to Solomon Traum in December of 1918, one month after the end of the war. As you can see, the place to which the visa was granted was the Bucovina."

"Does that mean that the Bucovina was the only place they could go?"

"No, they were free to go anywhere. The document I gave you previously shows that Solomon Traum was born in the year 1870, in the Bucovina. It was from there he came to Vienna in 1913, the year before the war began."

Robert sifted through the pile of papers, removed a sheet and read it.

"That is why the exit visa was issued to the Bucovina," explained the clerk, "even though this region, having before the war been part of Austria, belonged following the war to Romania."

"I thought that the Bucovina was divided between Romania and Ukraine?"

"It is now. During World War II, it belonged to Germany, and after that it was divided between the Soviet Union and Romania. Since the break-up of the U.S.S.R., the northern Bucovina is in Ukraine. The southern half remains the property of Romania."

"So we don't really know the details of the Traum family's emigration to America."

The clerk shook his head. "There is one other thing: Solomon Traum's profession, listed in the Vienna directory of 1917, was recorded as 'Printer.' On the ground floor of number five Zirkusgasse was located a printer's shop. Other than this, we have no useful information.

"The son of Solomon Traum was a very important writer?"

"He was a novelist," Robert said. "I believe most of his books have been translated into German."

The clerk shrugged his shoulders. "I never read novels. The only fiction I read is in the newspapers."

Robert stood up and put on his coat.

"Thank you for your help," he said.

"And where do you go now?"

"To Romania. But first, I want to see the house in Leopoldstadt."

The clerk raised his right index finger. "Wait a moment," he said.

The clerk disappeared into another room, then reemerged carrying a book. He opened it, located a particular page and placed the book in Robert's hands.

"Here is a photograph of Zirkusgasse at the turn of the century," the clerk told him. "Many of these houses have been destroyed and new buildings constructed. It's possible that number five no longer resembles what you see in this photograph."

Robert inspected the photograph, then handed the book back to the clerk.

"I'll let you know."

The clerk snapped the book closed, and said, "If you like."

5.

ROBERT STOOD IN FRONT OF NUMBER FIVE ZIRKUSGASSE. It was, indeed, no longer the house that appeared in the photograph. In place of the brick building was an ugly cement block of apartments that had been constructed sometime during the 1970s. The snow was now only flurrying. Robert turned away and walked a short distance to the river. He proceeded onto a footbridge, stopped and leaned against the railing. Robert watched as barges and small boats plied the icy water.

6.

ROBERT STOOD AT THE AIRLINE INFORMATION COUNTER in the airport in Bucharest, his suitcase on the floor next to him. Above the desk was a sign in Romanian, Italian, English, French, German and Japanese: "Welcome to Bucharest."

"There are no airports close to where you want to go," said the man behind the counter. "You will be better off going by train."

"Thank you," said Robert.

He picked up his suitcase and walked away.

7.

ROBERT, A DRINK IN FRONT OF HIM, WAS SEATED AT THE bar of the Bucharest Kapitol Hotel. On the bar next to his drink was a stack of bills. There was a moderate amount of activity in the bar, which kept the bartender just busy enough. An attractive, well-dressed young woman took a seat on the stool next to Robert's. She took out a cigarette and lit it. The bartender brought her a drink and set it in front of her without comment, then walked away.

She took a sip of her drink, then turned toward Robert and asked, *"Sei solo?"*

Robert shook his head. *"Non parlo Italiano. Sono Americano."*

"I'm sorry," said the woman, "there are many Italian people coming for business now to Romania."

"I'm not a businessman."

"No, what do you do?"

"I'm a writer. I've come to do research for a book."

The woman almost smiled. "I don't believe you. Foreign men come here for only the gold mines and the girls."

Other women, most of them probably prostitutes, some on the arms of men, passed through the bar.

"Gold mines?" said Robert. "I didn't know there were gold mines in Romania."

The woman took a long drag on her long cigarette, exhaled, then replied, "In the North. You have heard of the Carpathian Mountains? Dracula?"

"I didn't know he was in the mining business."

They both sipped their drinks.

"There are many beautiful women in Bucharest," Robert said, "including yourself."

"Our country is full of beautiful women, every one of them dying to leave. There is nothing for them here."

"Why are you here?"

"Without enough money, it is difficult to leave. The most common way to escape is to marry an Italian businessman. Another is to become a mistress of a Turk."

The woman put her cigarette out in an ashtray on the bar and slid off of her stool.

"You will pay for my drink?" she asked.

"Sure."

The woman looked directly into Robert's eyes and said, "You have come to a place I think you will not understand, or forget. It is almost oriental."

She walked away. The bartender came over, picked

up all of the bills from the bar that were in front of Robert and put them into his vest pocket.

"Something else?" he asked.

8.

ROBERT WAS SEATED IN A COMPARTMENT ON A TRAIN, NEXT to a window. There were very few other passengers, none of whom spoke to him. Robert looked out the window and studied the wintry landscape. As the train passed through small villages, Robert saw Gypsy families in horse-drawn carts on the roads, birch forests, Gypsy palaces with silver zinc minarets and Chinese pagoda-like roofs. Cars on the road were mostly pokey old Dacias being passed occasionally by fancy Italian automobiles going very fast. Abandoned factories from the Communist era appeared like ugly ghosts, rotting in the weeds.

The train passed over and through the Carpathian Mountains. A horse suddenly appeared from a mountain path pulling a single log followed by a man carrying an axe trotting after it. The train's progression through the mountains became more harrowing. Several times the train's progress was halted while workers shoveled snow off the tracks or cleared away fallen tree limbs. At one point, Robert saw a sign warning of the presence of wolves and bears, which were represented by a drawing of each.

Robert walked through the rainy streets of a big Eastern European city at night. Dully lit signs in an indecipherable language flashed on and off. Robert appeared desperate, frightened. He stopped a passerby, a man.

"I'm looking for my hotel. Can you help?" Robert asked him.

The man brushed Robert off and walked away. Robert continued searching through the streets. The rain came down harder.

The train lurched to a halt. Robert woke up, realizing that he had been asleep; he'd been dreaming. A conductor walked down the aisle toward him.

"Why did the train stop?" Robert asked the conductor.

"Moment," the conductor replied. "Stay tonight in Cosna. Not go, not go."

The train started moving backwards in the direction from which it had come.

Soon the train pulled into the station at Cosna.

Robert and the other passengers disembarked. The conductor stood on the platform, looked at Robert and pointed his finger past the station house.

"Hotel there," he said.

Robert pointed to his watch and asked, "What time do we leave?"

"*Dimineata*. Morning."

9.

INSIDE A SMALL HOTEL ROOM, ROBERT, STILL CLOTHED, was lying on a narrow bed with his eyes closed.

Robert walked through the rainy streets of a big Eastern European city. He felt desperate. A ghoulish version of the attractive woman with whom he spoke in the hotel bar in Bucharest appeared suddenly by his side. She linked one of her arms through his. Robert broke away from her. Two large, thuggish-looking men began following him. Robert walked faster, as did the men.

There was a loud knock on the door. Robert woke up, startled.

"Yes?"

A voice from the other side of the door announced, *"Trenul!"*

10.

ROBERT WAS LOOKING OUT THE WINDOW AS THE TRAIN slowed to a stop. The station sign read, SUCEAVA. Robert grabbed his bags and exited his compartment.

He stood on the platform, holding his suitcase. The few passengers who had also disembarked quickly disappeared, leaving Robert standing alone on the platform. He saw a taxi stand and walked toward it. There was one taxi cab waiting. As Robert approached, the taxi drove away. He watched it go.

Rain began to fall, softly at first, then harder. Robert stood under the overhanging roof of the station house. Two bearded men wearing turbans came out of the station house, gesturing and speaking to one another in a language Robert could not understand. He stepped in front of them.

"Suceava?" asked Robert.

The men stopped and stared at him.

"I need to get to Suceava, the City Hall. Can you help me?"

The rain came down harder.

One of the men replied in English, "We will take you there."

11.

THE TWO TURBANED MEN SAT IN THE FRONT SEAT OF a Renault sedan. Robert, holding his suitcase, sat in the back.

The man in the front passenger seat turned and said to Robert, "I have a cousin living in Oakland, California. He owns a fleet of taxis. He is always sending money back to our village in Tadzhikistan."

The driver turned and said, "You've come very far."

"You've obviously come a long way, too," said Robert.

"You are here for business?" asked the man in the front passenger seat.

"For information. I'm searching for someone's birthplace."

"Not your own?" asked the driver.

"No."

"A man has a great many birthplaces," said the other man. "Too many to count."

They rode the rest of the way in silence.

12.

THE RAIN STOPPED. ROBERT STOOD WITH HIS SUITCASE on the sidewalk. The two turbaned men drove away. Robert looked around. The buildings were mostly unadorned, Soviet-style structures. He walked up the steps and into the City Hall building.

Robert was seated alone at a table. There was nothing in the room, absolutely nothing, except for a metal table and two metal chairs. There was one smoked-glass window that admitted muted light.

The door opened and a woman entered, carrying a notepad and a pen. She sat down in the chair on the other side of the table from Robert. She was in her early- to mid-thirties, quite beautiful but conservatively dressed. Her appearance was the opposite of ostentatious. She studied Robert for several seconds before she spoke.

"You do not speak Romanian, Mr. Botto?"

"No, I have some French but it's not very good."

"No matter, I speak English. My name is Tanya Georgescu."

Tanya looked at her notebook.

"You are investigating a family by the name of 'Traum'?" she asked.

"I'm looking for the birthplace of the son of Solomon Traum. The American novelist, Rudolph Traum."

"You are professor?"

"Yes, at Stanford University, in California."

"He is very important, this novelist? I have never heard of him."

"He was a great writer but not so popular. His books have been translated into many languages."

"But not into Romanian."

"Not that I know of. He died last year."

"He was young?"

"No, he was eighty-two. He lived most of his adult life in Chicago."

"You look like you are tired, Mr. Botto."

"I am, and hungry, too. I just got off the train from Cosna."

"There is nothing in Cosna."

"Look, could I buy you lunch? I really do think I need to eat. I feel a little weak."

"I do not see why not. It is time."

Tanya stood up, as did Robert.

"Perhaps you could give me the name of a good hotel," asked Robert.

"No, that is impossible."

Robert stared at Tanya.

"There are no good hotels in Suceava," she continued. "But you will find something."

Tanya exited the room. Robert followed her.

13.

TANYA AND ROBERT WERE SEATED AT A TABLE, EATING and drinking.

"Your daughter is how old?" said Tanya.

"She's eight," said Robert.

"My father died when I was seven. My mother remarried two years later."

"Are you married?"

"I was, for a short time. It was not a good match."

"No children?"

"No, not yet."

"You're still very young."

"Not very young, but there is hope, I think."

"It's hard to believe that I'm here, in the Bucovina."

"Why?"

"It just seems strange to be doing what Buddy Traum meant to do, but never did."

"Perhaps it is you who is meant to be here."

They continued to eat and drink.

14.

ROBERT WALKED OUT OF HIS HOTEL AND ACCIDENTALLY bumped into a passerby, an older man, perhaps in his sixties. The older man turned and shouted at Robert in Romanian. He was extremely hostile.

"I'm sorry," said Robert, "I didn't see you."

The older man continued to yell at Robert as he walked away. Robert could do nothing but stare after him.

15.

ROBERT WAS SEATED AT THE SAME TABLE, IN THE SAME room in the City Hall building as he had been when he first met Tanya. Tanya entered, wearing the same conservative outfit that she had worn the day before, carrying a sheaf of papers. She sat down opposite Robert. Tanya hardly glanced at him and began looking through the papers. She did not seem happy.

"Maybe this was a bad idea," said Robert.

Tanya looked up at him.

"Not at all. Solomon Traum was a Jew, yes?"

"Yes."

"You told me yesterday that Solomon Traum was from southern Bucovina. The Jews were mostly residents of two towns, Radauti and Siret. Virtually the entire Jewish population of this part of the Bucovina was wiped out during World War II by the Nazis. Some of those who escaped fled to Moldavia, which was not invaded by the Germans. Others went north, into Ukraine and deeper into Russia. Of course, many of those were later murdered by Stalin. I believe that the family Traum came from one of these two places, Radauti or Siret. I suggest you look first in Radauti."

Tanya stood up, holding the papers in her arms. Robert stood up as well.

"Well, thank you," he said. "What is the easiest way for me to get to Radauti?"

"By car. There is no good train service."

Tanya studied Robert's face.

"I have a car. I will take you," she said.

"How can you leave your job?"

"You are my job now. You are doing legitimate research, and it is the duty of the department to assist you."

"Not everybody in Suceava has been as nice to me as you have."

Tanya smiled slightly.

"How do you know I am being nice?" she said.

16.

TANYA DROVE. ROBERT SAT NEXT TO HER IN THE FRONT passenger seat.

"I make less than one hundred dollars a month," Tanya said.

"Is that really enough for you to live on?"

"Since the fall of the regime, living conditions have

improved only a very little. Before, even though the quality of life was not very good, people had the security of knowing they would be taken care of by the state. Now, they have no such feeling. In some ways, it is a more difficult time. You are fortunate to have such a secure position at a prestigious university."

"You're right, I'm spoiled. I guess one of the reasons I'm here is because I'm restless. I needed an adventure."

"Here, to have an adventure perhaps means something different than it does in America"

"What is that?" asked Robert.

"An adventure for a man or a woman means to have a little romance, something temporary, a brief excitement. And then you go home, back to your normal life."

"It's not what I had in mind but it doesn't sound so terrible," said Robert.

They both laughed. Robert looked out the window and saw the city limits sign for Radauti.

17.

TANYA AND ROBERT DROVE SLOWLY IN HER CAR DOWN A little street. The car stopped and they got out.

"I'm certain this is the street they told us to look," said Tanya.

"What is the woman's name?"

"Oana Koppelman. She is the keeper of the archive regarding the history of the Jews in the Bucovina."

Tanya stopped a man walking toward them on the street.

"Can you help me?" she asked him, in Romanian. "I am looking for number eleven but not all of the houses here have numbers."

"An old Jewish woman lives there," he said, and pointed to a small apartment building. "It's across the street, the one with the yellow door."

"*Multumesc*," said Tanya.

Tanya and Robert crossed the street and knocked on the yellow door. A woman in her seventies opened it.

"You are Oana Koppelman?" Tanya asked her.

"Yes, I've been expecting you. Come in."

18.

TANYA AND ROBERT WERE SEATED ON A SMALL COUCH IN front of a table upon which rested several large books. Oana sat in a chair opposite them.

"I have no record of a family named Traum in Radauti," said Oana. "The Jews here, before World War II, spoke mostly Yiddish. In Siret, they spoke High German."

"Buddy wrote in *The Phantom Father* that his father spoke German, not Yiddish," said Robert.

"Then they probably came from Siret. I know a man there who might be able to help you, Sami Grinberg. He operates the local cinema. He is in his eighties now."

The telephone rang.

"Excuse me," said Oana.

She got up, went over to the telephone and picked up the receiver. She listened for a few seconds, then hung up. She came back to her chair and sat down.

"This happens six times a day. They are always checking up on me. I don't even know why I bother to answer the telephone anymore."

"Who is 'they'?" asked Robert.

"*Securitate.* Secret police."

"*Securitate?* I thought they were expunged with the fall of Ceausescu."

"There is still the regime," said Tanya.

"My sister, Anca, lives in Siret," said Oana. "You have

a car? I can go with you in the morning to introduce you to Sami."

Tanya stood up.

"We will be here at ten," she said.

19.

ROBERT AND TANYA SAT IN THE DIMLY LIT BAR OF THEIR hotel, having drinks.

"Do you see that man over there?" Tanya asked.

Robert looked in the direction to which Tanya indicated.

"The one who looks like Hoagy Carmichael?"

"Ho-gie?"

"Do you know who James Bond is?"

"Of course. Sean Connery."

"Before the films, James Bond was a character in novels by Ian Fleming. Fleming described Bond as resembling Hoagy Carmichael, who looked nothing like Sean Connery. Hoagy Carmichael was a singer and songwriter in the 1930s and '40s. He wrote 'Stardust.' Anyway, what about that man?"

"He is *Securitate,* I am sure of it. He looks at us."

"Why would we be of interest to him?"

"They prefer to keep track of everyone."

"But you work for the government."

"That is even more reason for them to pay attention."

Tanya sipped her drink.

"It is not the same in America?" she asked.

"I don't know. It's just not so common."

Robert lifted his glass and drank.

20.

ROBERT AND TANYA WALKED DOWN THE CORRIDOR toward Tanya's room. They stopped in front of her door. Tanya took out a key and opened it. Before entering, she turned and looked at Robert. They stood silently for a moment, then Tanya took his hand and shook it firmly.

"Eight-thirty for breakfast," she said.

She turned and entered the room, shutting the door behind her.

21.

THE NEXT DAY THE WEATHER WAS UNSEASONABLY WARM and sunny. The car carrying Robert, Tanya and Oana was on the way to Siret. Tanya was driving. They came to a bend in the road.

"Can you stop the car, please?" Robert said.

Tanya pulled the car to the side of the road and stopped. Robert got out.

It was a particularly beautiful spot, surrounded by birch trees, their branches waving in the breeze. A small stream flowed nearby. Narrow gauge railroad tracks crossed the road. Off to one side was an enormous Gypsy palace. On the front porch, a woman was brushing out and drying her just-washed, waist-length black hair. Tanya got out of the car, walked over and stood next to Robert.

"This is a lovely place," he said.

"You prefer the countryside to the city?"

"I need both, don't you?"

Walking along the other side of the road, headed in the opposite direction, was a young Gypsy girl, perhaps fifteen or sixteen, wrapped in a silver-and-black-striped strapless dress, wearing high heels and big sunglasses. Her long, cobalt hair was being blown back by the wind. She walked past without a glance at or word to Robert and Tanya.

"That girl—" said Robert

"A Gypsy. What about her?"

"Not what I expected to see on a lonely road through the Carpathian mountains. She could be on a runway in Milan."

"Perhaps she will, one day."

After a few moments, they got back into the car. Tanya began to drive.

"Most of the time these big, ugly houses are empty," said Oana. "The Gypsies are in Germany, begging on the streets."

Tanya drove on.

22.

TANYA'S CAR THREADED ITS WAY THROUGH THE LITTLE streets of Siret and came to a stop in front of a movie theater. Tanya, Robert and Oana got out of the car.

"This is where Sami Grinberg works," said Oana.

They walked to the entrance and saw that it was padlocked. Next door to the theater in the same building was a small music school. Sounds of students practicing were audible. Oana walked over and knocked on the door. A woman opened the door.

"We are looking for Sami Grinberg," said Oana, "the man who operates the cinema. Do you know him?"

"Sami has gone to Moldavia," said the woman, "to visit relatives. I am the music teacher here."

"Do you know when he comes back?"

"He has been gone already a few weeks. He should be back soon, any day."

"Unless he's dead."

"Yes, unless he's dead."

"He's old, you know," said Oana.

"So are you," said the music teacher.

The woman closed the door. Oana walked back over to Tanya and Robert and told them, "Sami is away but she thinks he will return soon. We can go to my sister's house."

The three of them climbed back into Tanya's car and drove away.

23.

OANA'S YOUNGER SISTER, ANCA, LIVED ALONE. HER apartment was small and crowded with furniture and antique objects. The sisters and Tanya and Robert were seated at the dining room table, having lunch. Anca picked up a bowl and ladled a large spoonful of its contents onto Robert's plate.

"More polenta," she said.

"Thank you," said Robert, "but I've already eaten too much."

"If it's good, you can't eat too much," said Oana.

"Do you like it?" asked Anca.

"Yes, it's very good," said Robert.

"Then eat," said Oana.

"What about you?" Anca asked Tanya.

Tanya offered up her plate.

"I will have some more," she said.

Anca ladled polenta onto Tanya's plate.

"A real man does not desire a woman who is too thin," said Oana.

"Is that right, Mr. Robert?" said Anca. "I heard that in America all of the women are too thin."

"Not all of them," said Robert.

"I will stay here with my sister until the day after tomorrow," said Oana. "Then Anca will come with me on the bus to Radauti. If you wish to remain in Siret, and wait for Sami to return, there are a couple of hotels that are not too bad."

"I'll stay," replied Robert. "I'm sure I'll be all right here by myself."

"I will stay also," said Tanya, looking at Robert. "As I told you, this is my job."

Tanya and Robert were leaving, putting on their coats. Oana and Tanya were off to one side. Anca helped Robert on with his coat and then whispered to him, "Tanya *Securitate.*"

Before Robert could respond, Tanya came over and together they thanked Anca and Oana for their hospitality and then left the apartment.

24.

ROBERT AND TANYA STROLLED ALONG THE STREETS OF Siret. A light snow was falling. It was very cold.

"So you first read the novels of Buddy . . ."

"When I was eighteen," said Robert. "I read two that year: His most famous, *The Enchanted,* and its sequel, *The Disenchanted.*"

"You like them why?"

"I thought they were about man's inhumanity to man and how the world could be changed for the better."

"You thought?"

"I was thirty before I read the novels again, and I realized then that I had thoroughly misunderstood them. Traum wasn't writing about man's being able to change the world, he was writing about it changing despite man."

"Are you happy with your work?"

"I'm fairly well paid, I live in a nice place."

"This does not answer my question," said Tanya.

They came upon a person wrapped in a large overcoat, lying half on the sidewalk and half in the street. Other pedestrians ignored the body, and walked swiftly past it. Tanya and Robert stopped. Robert squatted down and turned the person over, revealing the bearded face of a middle-aged man. The man's eyes were closed.

"He is dead?" said Tanya.

"No, just passed out drunk. We should get him inside before he freezes to death, though."

The man opened his eyes and looked at Robert. Then he looked at Tanya. He smiled and closed his eyes again.

"Robert, you must move!" said Tanya.

She took Robert by the arm and pulled him up.

"What is it?" he said.

He looked down and saw that the man was urinating. Urine ran down his pants leg onto the snow in the spot where Robert had been squatting.

"He will not freeze now," said Tanya.

She put her arm through Robert's, and they walked on.

25.

TANYA AND ROBERT STOOD IN FRONT OF THE STILL-padlocked front door of the movie theater. They walked away. As they were leaving, the music teacher approached them, walking briskly on the same side of the street. She nodded to them as she passed.

26.

AS BAD DISCO MUSIC POUNDED, ROBERT AND TANYA SAT at a table in the Bar Paris, observing a few not particularly energetic couples working out on the dance floor. A waitress brought drinks for them. Tanya paid her. Robert attempted to pay, but Tanya stopped him. The waitress left.

"In America, the man always pays?"

"Usually, yes," said Robert.

"Usually in Romania, also. You prefer that I am unusual, yes?"

Before Robert could answer, two heavy-set men, both bald and bearded, who could have been anywhere from thirty to fifty years old, walked up to Tanya and Robert's table. They sat down at the table in two chairs opposite Tanya and Robert.

"This friendly place," said one of the men. "We sitting okay?"

"Help yourself," said Robert.

"Da," he said, signaling for the waitress, who came over.

He looked at the waitress, pointed to himself and said, "Vodka." He then pointed to his companion and said, "Vodka."

Finally, he pointed with two fingers of the same hand, index and pinky, to Tanya and Robert.

"We're all right, thank you," said Robert.

The man motioned to the waitress that she could leave.

"I am Vitali. This is Vladimir."

"Robert." And then, nodding toward Tanya, he said, "Tanya."

Vladimir asked Tanya, "It is okay to dance?"

"Certainly, this is a disco," she said.

Vladimir smiled and stood up. Tanya did not move. Vladimir stopped smiling and sat down. The waitress came back and set drinks down in front of Vladimir and Vitali. Vitali paid her and then said to the waitress, in Russian, "What time do you get off?"

The waitress replied, in Russian, "I'll get off, but not with you."

She left.

"Women here are not so friendly as in Ukraine," said Vitali.

"Is that where you're from?" asked Robert.

"*Da*. Kiev."

He and Vladimir knocked back their vodkas.

Tanya said to Vitali, in Russian, "You have another chance with the waitress now."

Vladimir laughed. Vitali, unsmiling, stared at Tanya.

"You have business with Sami Grinberg?" he said.

"How did you know we were looking for him?" asked Robert.

"He is with us," said Vladimir.

"With you?" said Robert.

"He is our business partner," said Robert.

"You can talk to us," said Vladimir.

"We are not here to do business," said Tanya.

Vitali turned to Robert and said, "You are American?"

"Yes."

"No Americans in Siret," said Vladimir. "You are with government?"

"No."

"He does research for a book about a writer whose father was from the Bucovina," said Tanya.

"What writer?" said Vitali.

"Rudolph Traum," said Robert. "Sami Grinberg may have some information about his family."

"Have you read him?" Tanya asked.

Vitali ignored the question and looked around for the waitress.

"I did not think so," said Tanya.

Vladimir noticed several girls sitting at a nearby table. He stood up.

"I go dance," he said.

He went over to talk to the girls.

Tanya leaned toward Robert.

"I think it is better we leave now," she said.

She and Robert stood up. The waitress came over. Tanya glanced at the waitress and then nodded at Vitali. *"Dos vedanya,"* she said.

27.

ROBERT AND TANYA STOOD IN FRONT OF HER HOTEL room door.

"I guess Siret is like any small town," said Robert.

"How?" asked Tanya.

"Everybody knows everybody else's business, or wants to know."

"So, good night."

"We've been here before. In front of your door, I mean."

Tanya looked into his eyes for a moment, then kissed him on the cheek. She turned with her room key in her hand and opened the door, then turned back to look at Robert.

"You didn't do that before," he said.

"Did not do what? Kiss you on your cheek?"

"Turn and look at me again."

He kissed Tanya on the lips, then embraced her and kissed her a second time. This time, she responded.

After this kiss, Robert was eager for more, but Tanya put two fingers to his mouth, turned away and quickly went inside and closed the door. Robert reluctantly moved away from the door and walked down the hallway. In front of several of the doors were shoes, left by guests to be shined before the morning. Robert kicked one of the shoes, then went over and picked it up and returned it to its place. He walked away.

28.

IT WAS SNOWING AS ROBERT AND TANYA WAITED AT THE bus stop with Oana and Anca. A bus was parked next to the curb. They were standing beneath a small shelter. Oana handed a letter to Robert.

"This you give to Sami Grinberg," she told him. "I explain why you are here."

"And this is for you," replied Robert.

He handed her some money.

"This is for the bus, and something extra," he said. "Thank you for your help."

Oana took the money and put it in a pocket.

"I hope you find what you are looking for," she said.

Oana and Robert shook hands. The bus driver arrived, opened the door of the bus and began taking tickets from the passengers, who then boarded the bus.

Tanya and Oana shook hands. Anca shook Robert's hand and said to him, "Romanian women are not so thin as the American."

"I don't know," said Robert.

"You will," said Anca.

Anca shook hands with Tanya, and then Oana and Anca got on the bus. They were the last passengers to board. The bus driver climbed in, closed the door and drove away.

29.

VITALI AND VLADIMIR SAT ACROSS FROM THE MAYOR OF Siret, Lucian Clujescu, who was seated behind his desk in his dark office. Outside a large window behind the mayor, snow fell steadily.

"Are you certain of the name?" asked Clujescu.

"Traum," replied Vitali. "That was the family."

"And this Robert?"

"He says he's writing a book about the son."

"There is a woman with him," said Vladimir.

"American?" asked Clujescu.

"No, Romanian," said Vitali.

"She speaks good Russian," added Vladimir.

"Do you know her name?"

"Tanya," said Vladimir.

"My impression is that she is with him in some official capacity," said Vitali.

"Why do you think this?"

"She wouldn't dance with me," said Vladimir.

"Grinberg is still away?"

"I think so," said Vitali. "He should be back any time now. Should we be worried?"

"The properties on which are located the cinema and the old synagogue once belonged to the Traum family. This was before World War I. Solomon Traum leased it to Sami Grinberg's father."

"But surely it was nationalized," said Vitali.

"This guy Robert could be a lawyer representing the Traum family in America," said Vladimir. "Perhaps they want to reclaim the properties."

"Our deal is with Grinberg," said Vitali.

"He holds the deeds," said the mayor, "but since the end of the regime there is a question about the ownership."

"You promised that we could begin developing the property in the spring," said Vitali.

"With the proper permits, yes."

Vitali stood up, followed by Vladimir.

"You have been paid for the permits."

"Don't worry, Vitali, I will take care of it."

"We will take care of it, too," said Vitali.

Mayor Clujescu stood up.

"Be careful, Vitali, this woman . . ."

"Tanya," said Vladimir.

"Most likely she is *Securitate,*" Clujescu said.

"I know what I am doing," said Vitali.

Vitali and Vladimir turned to go.

"Remember, this is Romania, not Ukraine."

"How can we forget?" said Vladimir. "The weather is so much better here."

Vladimir and Vitali left the mayor's office.

30.

ROBERT WAS ALONE IN HIS HOTEL ROOM. HE WAS speaking on the telephone.

"Hello, sweetheart.

"Yes, I am.

"It's very cold, and snowing hard.

"I wish I were, too. It won't be very long.

"He did? No, your mother didn't tell me.

"Of course it's all right with me.

"No, I don't need to talk to her.

"I will.

"A snowman? I haven't seen one yet. Just a lot of men covered with snow.

"I love you, Rebecca. I'll call again soon.

"Bye, honey."

Robert hung up the phone and went over to the window and looked out at the snow. The telephone rang. He walked over and picked it up.

"Hello?"

There was a knock at the door.

"Just a minute," Robert said into the receiver, "there's someone at the door."

He put the phone down, and went and opened the door. It was Tanya.

"Come in," said Robert.

Tanya entered. Robert closed the door.

"You should never do that," she said.

"What?"

"Open the door before asking who is there. It is not always me."

"Excuse me, I have someone on the phone."

Robert picked up the receiver.

"Hello, I'm sorry, I—"

He listened for a moment, then hung up.

"Who was there?" asked Tanya.

"Nobody. I mean there was, before you knocked. It was a man."

"What did he want?"

"I don't know. I didn't have a chance to ask. Please, sit down."

Tanya sat down on the end of the bed.

"I am afraid there will be some trouble," she said.

Robert sat down on the bed near her.

"About what?"

"It is hard to believe you are here only for the writing of a book."

"What else would I be doing here? I don't know anyone. I can't speak Romanian."

He paused and looked directly at Tanya.

"Is this what you came to tell me?" he asked her.

"Yes."

"You mean, it's you who doesn't believe me."

"Did you find your daughter?"

"Yes, I spoke with her. She's all right."

"You are worried about her?"

Robert stood up, moved away, stopped, then looked back at Tanya.

"You know, I'm alone here. And sometimes, even when I am with you, I feel as if I were alone."

"You feel alone with me?"

"Tanya, I don't know who you are or even why you're with me. Not really."

Tanya stood up.

"You are hungry? I am suddenly."

Robert stared at Tanya for a moment, then walked back over to her.

"Then let's go to dinner," he said.

"I must get some things."

She went to the door, opened it and walked out, leaving the door open. Robert took his overcoat out of the closet, draped it over his arm and followed her. He closed the door behind him.

After a moment, the telephone rang. It continued to ring.

31.

SAMI GRINBERG WAS A SMALL MAN IN HIS LATE SEVENTIES or early eighties, but he was still strong and full of life. He wore a cowboy hat and a heavy coat and carried a suitcase. He stopped in front of the door to his apartment, put down the suitcase, took out a key, opened the door, picked up the suitcase and went inside.

The apartment was dark. Sami entered, put down his suitcase and was about to close the door when he saw the red-yellow glow of a burning cigarette ash in his living room.

"Close the door, Sami. You weren't raised in a barn, were you? Or, come to think of it, maybe you were."

Sami turned on a light and saw Mayor Clujescu seated in a chair in the living room, smoking a cigarette. Standing next to the mayor was a tall, slender man dressed in a dark suit. The tall, slender man had one hand in one of his jacket pockets and stared intently at Sami. Sami closed the door, then walked slowly into the living room and stopped. He stood there, staring at Clujescu.

"Who let you in?" said Sami. "And what are you doing here?"

"I like your hat, Sami. It suits you. A real *Yiddish* cowboy."

"You're not here to talk about my hat."

Clujescu stood up.

"In fact, I'm not here at all. And neither is Tudor. Are you, Tudor?"

Tudor remained silent.

"I didn't think so," said the mayor.

"I'm tired," said Sami. "Get to the point."

"You made a promise to the Ukrainians. I'm here to remind you to keep it."

"What business is this of yours? I didn't make any promises to anyone."

Tudor walked over to Sami and with his free hand started to remove Sami's hat from his head. Sami kicked Tudor in the balls. Tudor grunted and doubled over. Sami replaced his cowboy hat properly on his head. Tudor straightened up, pulled a pistol out of his coat pocket and shoved the business end of the barrel into Sami's left ear.

"Still a fighter, huh, Sami?" said Clujescu. "You should be with the rest of your people, murdering Palestinians."

"Your grandfather would be proud of you."

"Remember what I said about keeping your promise. Let's go, Tudor."

Tudor took the nose of his pistol out of Sami's ear and

with it flicked the hat off of Sami's head. The hat fell to the floor. Tudor and Clujescu walked out of the apartment, leaving the door open. Half a moment later, the mayor returned and placed a hand on the outside doorknob.

"*I* was not raised in a barn," he said, closing the door.

Sami listened to Clujescu and Tudor's footsteps disappearing down the hall. He bent down, picked up his hat, brushed it off and placed it gently on a table.

32.

ROBERT ENTERED THE MEN'S RESTROOM OF THE RESTAURANT in which he and Tanya were dining, went into a toilet stall and closed the door. He unzipped his trousers and dropped them around his feet as he sat on the toilet.

Vladimir entered the men's room and looked around. He and Robert were the only ones there. Vladimir walked over to Robert's toilet stall and leaned against the door.

Robert looked down and saw Vladimir's shoes through the space below the toilet stall door.

Robert coughed. Vladimir did not move. Robert coughed a second time. Vladimir took out a cigarette and lit it. Vladimir leisurely smoked his cigarette, flicking the ash on the floor by his feet.

Robert noticed the ash from Vladimir's cigarette fall on the floor just outside the stall door.

Tanya was seated at a table for two, smoking a cigarette, waiting for Robert to return. Vitali walked up to the table and sat down in Robert's chair. Tanya and he stared at each other. A waiter came over with a bottle of wine and said to Vitali, "Shall I pour it, sir?"

"Please."

The waiter poured wine in glasses set on the table in front of both Vitali and Tanya.

"Thank you," Vitali said to the waiter.

Vitali picked up his glass and extended it toward Tanya. She did not touch her glass.

"Narok!" he said.

"What do you want?" asked Tanya.

Vitali withdrew his arm and took a sip of the wine. He put the glass down.

"Sami Grinberg will not be coming back for a long time. Tell your friend Robert that things do not work the same here as they do in America."

"What do you know about how things work in America? And this is Romania, not Ukraine."

"Perhaps you and I could be of help to one another."

Tanya smoked, looked in the direction of the men's room, then at Vitali.

"Robert is coming back. You are in his chair."

"Don't worry, I will leave if he arrives."

"I am here," said Robert.

Vitali turned around and saw Robert standing behind him. Vitali stood up and said to Robert, "I was just, how do you say it, keeping warm your chair."

Robert picked up the glass of wine from which Vitali had been drinking and handed it to him.

"Finish your wine."

Vitali just looked at him.

"Finish it," said Robert.

Vitali drank the rest of the wine, then set the glass down on the table.

"Enjoy your dinner," he said.

Vitali turned and nodded at Tanya, then left. Robert sat down. The waiter came over.

"Would you bring me another glass, please?" Robert asked the waiter.

"Certainly, sir," replied the waiter.

Vladimir was bent over the sink in the men's room, washing his face. Vitali entered. Vladimir looked up into the mirror above the sink and saw Vitali. Vladimir had what appeared to be a red dent in his forehead. Vitali looked at Vladimir's reflection in the mirror.

"I ran into a door," said Vladimir.

Vitali turned around and left the men's room. Vladimir took a towel and dried off his face.

33.

ROBERT AND TANYA ENTERED THE LOBBY OF THEIR HOTEL.

"Shall we have a nightcap?" said Robert.

"Nightcap?"

"A drink before we go to bed."

"No, there are some things I must do. Anyway, I am tired."

She kissed him on both cheeks.

"Good night," she said.

"Good night."

Robert watched her go up the steps, then turned and entered the hotel bar.

Robert took a seat at the bar. Seated next to him was

a young couple, a man and a woman. The bartender came over to Robert and said, "Yes?"

Before Robert could order, the man seated with the girl interrupted.

"You are not Romanian?"

"No, I'm not," said Robert.

"Neither am I. I am Italian. You are American, yes?"

"Right again."

"You know Palinka? Romanian national drink. Very powerful. You must have it."

The Italian motioned to the bartender and said, "Bring him Palinka."

The bartender looked at Robert. Robert shrugged, the bartender turned away. The Italian extended his hand to Robert.

"My name is Guido," he said.

They shook hands.

"Someone told me about you," said Robert.

"Me? Who?"

"A woman in Bucharest."

Robert looked at the man's young female companion, who was very beautiful. She looked expressionlessly at Robert.

"What woman?" asked Guido.

"Never mind, I was only joking."

The bartender came back with a bottle of Palinka and a glass. He filled Robert's glass with a clear liquid, left the bottle on the bar and went away.

"What is your profession?" said Guido.

"I teach literature at a university."

"I am a manufacturer, of pants. I have a factory here." Guido picked up his glass and held it out toward Robert.

"What is your name?" he asked.

"Robert."

Robert picked up his glass. They touched glasses.

"Salute," said Guido.

"Salute."

They drank. Guido picked up the bottle and refilled Robert's glass. The girl next to Guido leaned in toward Robert and said, "Do you think Herman Melville meant for white whale to represent government?"

"What are you talking about?" Guido said to her.

"Moby-Dick," said Robert.

"Moby Dick? This might be a good name for a line of clothing. What do you think? For men, of course."

Robert looked back at the girl and said, "That's a

very logical question. It doesn't really matter what Melville meant, does it? Moby Dick could be a symbol for almost anything. It's Ahab's obsession."

"I would like to go to America," said the girl.

Guido put his arm around her possessively.

"First you must come to Milano," he told her.

The girl looked back at Robert.

"My first choice would be to go to America," she said. "Hollywood."

Guido snapped back at her in Italian, "Can't you stop being a whore?"

The girl responded, "In America, I wouldn't have to be a whore. I could get married."

They continued arguing in Italian. Robert finished his second glass of Palinka, put some money on the bar and left. The couple continued to argue and did not even notice that Robert had gone.

34.

AFTER LEAVING THE HOTEL BAR, ROBERT DECIDED TO TAKE a walk. He felt light-headed from the Romanian liquor. He stopped and steadied himself against a lamppost. He staggered forward and entered the same dream he had had on the train. Suddenly, Robert felt disoriented, lost.

A woman approached him and stopped directly in his path. He looked into her face, which was the face of a she-wolf.

The she-wolf spoke to Robert in Romanian: "Follow me," she commanded.

She turned and began walking. Robert followed her through the snowy streets. Finally, she stopped. The she-wolf turned and looked at Robert, who tried to kiss her. She laughed at him, turned and moved away. Robert realized that he was at the entrance to his hotel. He looked again for the she-wolf but she was gone. Then he saw in the distance a lone wolf running away in the snow into the darkness.

35.

TANYA AND ROBERT SAT AT A TABLE IN THEIR HOTEL dining room, having breakfast.

"You stayed up very late?" said Tanya.

"I'm not sure. I met an Italian businessman and his girlfriend in the bar. I think I drank too much

Palinka. They got into an argument, so I left and took a walk."

"You were alone?"

"Yes, of course. But then I got lost and someone helped me find my way back to the hotel."

"A woman?"

"Sort of. I'm afraid to tell you."

"Why afraid? Tell me."

"It was a she-wolf."

"She-wolf?"

"A woman who looked like a wolf. In fact, she was a wolf. She led me here and before I could thank her, she ran off."

"This was the Palinka running off with your mind."

"It won't happen again," said Robert.

"We will see," said Tanya.

36.

After breakfast, Robert spoke with the concierge.

"Steam bath," Robert said to him. "Sauna."

"Sauna, yes," said the concierge, who then took out a card, wrote on it and handed it to Robert.

"Turn right out of hotel, then next street right," he told Robert. "Number seventeen. Sauna."

Robert followed the concierge's instructions and stopped in front of a door with a "17" on it. He tried to open it, but the door was locked. He pressed a buzzer next to the door. After a few moments, the door opened. A man wearing a red fez stood looking at Robert. Robert handed him the hotel card. The man took it and read what the concierge had written on it.

The man stared at Robert and said, "Sauna."

He stood aside and allowed Robert to enter. The man closed the door behind him and then led Robert down a dank, damp-smelling hallway. The man showed him into a kind of dressing room which was more like a boudoir than a locker room.

"How much?" Robert asked.

The man in the red fez hat said, "One million *lei*."

Robert took money from his pocket and held it out. The man extracted from Robert's hand several bills, then he motioned for Robert to get undressed. Robert did, folding his clothes neatly and laying them on a couch. The man handed Robert a large towel, which Robert wrapped around himself. It was cold in the room and Robert began to shiver. The man led Robert through a different door down another hallway, then opened a smoked glass door and motioned for Robert to enter this room.

Robert went through the door and the man closed it behind him. In the room was a large, shallow pool, beautifully tiled, as were the walls and floor. Through the steamy mist, Robert saw that sitting in the pool and on the steps around it were seven very large, obese women of various ages wearing one-piece bathing suits. They were chattering and laughing among themselves until they saw Robert, at which point they stopped talking and turned their attention to him. The women stared at Robert and he at them. A couple of them were dousing themselves with water, the others just sitting still. The room was extremely hot. Robert was unsure of what to do.

One of the women spoke to the others in Romanian. "They sent us a handsome one this time, girls."

Some of the other women laughed. One of them stood up, climbed out of the pool, came over to Robert and relieved him of his towel. She took him by the hand and led him into the pool, where the women immediately surrounded him.

37.

ROBERT AND TANYA WERE WALKING TOGETHER ON THE street toward the music school and cinema.

"What did you do today?" Tanya asked.

"I took a steam bath," said Robert.

"Steam bath?"

"A sauna. The concierge told me where to go."

"It was satisfactory?"

"I would have to say so, yes."

"As good as in America?"

"I don't think there's anything like it in America."

They walked up to the music school and entered.

38.

INSIDE THE MUSIC SCHOOL, YOUNG STUDENTS WERE packing up their instruments. The music teacher was talking to a young girl. She noticed Robert and Tanya standing just inside the front door. She finished talking to her student, then walked over to Robert and Tanya.

"You are still here. I hope you are enjoying your stay in Siret."

"It's been interesting," said Robert. "Actually, we're about to leave. Oana gave us this letter."

Robert removed a letter from his coat pocket

"It's for Sami Grinberg," Robert conintued. "We were hoping you could give it to him."

"Why not give it to him yourself? He has returned. I think now he is at the cinema. His office is in the pro-jection booth."

"Thank you, we will," said Tanya.

Tanya and Robert left the music school.

39.

INSIDE THE CINEMA, TANYA AND ROBERT CLIMBED THE stairs to the projection booth. At the top of the stairs, next to the projection room, was a small office. They stopped at the door, even though it was open. Through the open door, they could see a small, older man looking though some papers on the desk. Tanya knocked on the door.

The man answered in Romanian, "Yes, who is there?"

Tanya and Robert entered the little office. Posters of old movies were taped and tacked to the walls.

"We are here to see Sami Grinberg," Tanya said.

"What for?" said Sami. "Sami Grinberg is a busy man."

"We have a letter for him."

Sami looked Tanya and Robert over carefully. Robert stepped forward and handed Oana's letter to Sami. Sami opened the letter and read it to himself. Sami finished the letter and looked at Robert.

"Do you speak Romanian? Or German?"

"He is an American," said Tanya. "He speaks only English."

"I am not American," Sami said in English, "but I speak English, too. I learn it here, from cinema. This was my university, founded by my father, Nathan Grinberg. It was then called Excelsior. During regime name was changed to Maxim Gorki. Now is Cultural Arts Cinema. One day again will be Excelsior."

Tanya and Robert looked around at the old posters on the walls. Many of them were French and Italian.

"Oana says you are professor," Sami said to Robert.

"Yes, I'm doing research for a book, a biography of the writer Rudolph Traum. His family . . ."

"I know all this from letter. You want to know about father."

"Yes."

"You are Jew?"

"No."

Sami pointed at Tanya.

"You?" he said.

"No," said Tanya.

Sami stood up, went over to a poster on the wall and pointed to it. The film advertised on the poster was *Judgment at Nuremberg,* starring Spencer Tracy and Marlene Dietrich. Sami stared at the poster.

"My father, always he want to meet Marlene Dietrich. But never did. She knew from von Sternberg how to put light. No genius now in cinema. Good students, yes, but no genius since Fellini. All are dead. Nathan saw them all and because of him, me, too. Sixty-five years I am cinema technician."

Sami moved toward the door.

"Come," he said.

Sami led them out of his office into the adjacent projection booth, where two projectors were mounted.

"Since I am fifteen years old, I have best seat in classroom."

He touched the projector with his hand.

"I take you now to synagogue," he said.

40.

Tanya, Robert and Sami were walking down the steps in the cinema.

"Before Nazis came Siret, our family went in Moldavia," said Sami. "In Siret, they leave alive only four Jews: lawyer, optometrist, dentist and gynecologist. Only what they need. After war, my family come back."

They exited the cinema. Sami, Tanya and Robert crossed to the other side and stopped at a fence surrounding the old synagogue. The gate was padlocked. The synagogue had obviously been abandoned for years. The facade was in advanced disrepair.

"Do people still use this synagogue?" asked Robert.

"No. It was built before turn of old century. Names of Jewish families who live in Siret before first war were written on wall inside."

"It is open?" said Tanya.

"No," said Sami, "but I have key."

Sami took out a key and unlocked the padlock on the gate. The three of them advanced to the entrance of the synagogue, where Sami took out another key and unlocked the door. They went inside.

41.

It was very dusty inside the synagogue, the walls were crumbling, as was the ancient Torah. High on the walls all around were naturalistic but almost fantastical paintings, all in bright (or what once were bright) colors. It was not a very large room; there were no seats. Tanya and Robert gazed at the paintings, which were mostly covered by cobwebs. Sami was standing near the wall at the rear of the synagogue.

"Here are names," he said.

Robert and Tanya walked over to him. Etched on the wall were columns of names of the Jewish families of Siret prior to World War I. They were not listed alphabetically. Sami pointed to one of the names

"There," he said.

Robert and Tanya bent forward to see. Etched into the wall was the name "Solomon Traum."

"Amazing," said Robert. "So Siret probably was the birthplace of both Buddy and his father, Solomon."

Robert turned to Sami and said, "Mr. Grinberg, I have two more questions."

"Mr. Grinberg was Nathan. I am Sami."

"Why did the Traum family leave Siret for Vienna?

And why, after World War I ended, having been granted an exit visa back to the Bucovina, did they not return but instead go to America?"

"Many people left to go to Vienna," said Tanya. "It was then capital of Austria. There was more work, more opportunity."

"That is not why they left," said Sami, "or why they did not return to Siret. I tell you now about Rosebud."

"Rosebud?" said Tanya.

Robert removed a small camera and took a photograph of the name "Traum" etched on the wall.

"Orson Welles," Sami said to Tanya. "*Citizen Kane.* It was last word of dying man. You do not know this film?"

"No."

"It was the name written on a sled Kane had when he was a boy," said Robert. "A symbol of lost innocence, I suppose."

The three of them looked around the old synagogue. Mute winter light slanted in through the high windows. They were in a Temple of the Lost, surrounded by dust and spiderwebs. A couple of large rats scurried across the floor near them.

"I have something else now show you," said Sami. They left the synagogue.

42.

SAMI LED TANYA AND ROBERT DOWN A NARROW FLIGHT of stairs into the cinema basement and then along a dank, narrow, unlit passageway. Sami stopped in the passageway, forcing Robert and Tanya to stop, too. Sami took out a box of matches from a pocket in his coat and handed it to Tanya.

"Light one," he told her.

Sami knelt down as Tanya lit a match. He removed several bricks from the floor. From below, he removed a small metal box, which he handed to Robert. Sami then replaced the bricks on the floor. He stood up and took the box from Robert. Tanya blew out the match. Sami led them back through the passageway in the direction from which they had come.

Inside the theater itself, instead of row seating, there were, perhaps, sixty individual wooden chairs. Sami sat down in one of them, turning it before he did so to face two other chairs, upon which Robert and Tanya sat. Sami opened the metal box and removed from it a small-caliber pistol.

"This belong to Solomon Traum."

"How do you know this?" asked Tanya.

"This is reason Traum family leave Bucovina, could not return. I tell you story as my father, Nathan, told it me.

"Before first war, in Bucovina, was group called League of National Christian Defence. They hate especially Jews. Later, they become Legion of Archangel Michael, Iron Guard, used by Nazis. But before first war, they are same, want to take everything from Jews, to destroy. Leader in Siret of League of National Christian Defence was Alexandru Rakozi.

"One day winter," Sami told them, "Alexandru Rakozi march with several men in demonstration, carry signs identify them belong to League of National Christian Defence. Citizens line sidewalks, some cheer, some just watching. As demonstrators file by, one of crowd, tall man, forty years old, turn and walk away in opposite direction of marchers. This was young Solomon Traum. Two other men, about same age as Traum, join him. Together they turn backs on demonstrators.

"That night they meet at small café. Solomon Traum

and two men from demonstration, Andrei and Ferenc, sit at table drinking tea.

" 'To find Rakozi alone will not be so easy,' say Andrei.

" 'His Green Shirts are always with him,' say Ferenc.

" 'We have find out what he likes to do,' Traum tell them, 'what his private amusements are.'

" 'Other than terrorize Jewish shopkeepers, you mean,' say Ferenc.

" 'He has mistress,' say Andrei.

" 'Do you know who she is?' Traum ask.

" 'Yes, she is daughter of baker, Constanta.'

" 'We can get to Rakozi through girl,' Traum tell them. 'Find out when she goes with him, and where.'

" 'How do I find this out?' ask Andrei.

" 'Does your family eat bread?' say Traum.

"Andrei look at Traum and nod.

"Next day, Traum is working at letterpress when Andrei come.

" 'He take her to theater,' say Andrei.

" 'When?' ask Traum.

" 'Tomorrow night.'

" 'I go see Grinberg when finish here.'

"Andrei leave.

"At Excelsior next night, customers come to theater. Rakozi and mistress take seats. Traum enter, wearing black slouch hat, and take seat behind Rakozi. Traum remove hat and hold it in lap. Customers settle down and play begin. It is comedy during which duel is fought with pistols. Just before moment in play where pistols are fired, Traum remove from his coat a gun, which he conceal with hat. The pistols on stage are fired, following which audience erupt in big laughter. Rakozi slump down in seat, head hanging one side.

"His mistress laugh along with others, pay no attention to Rakozi. When she finally notice he is no longer conscious and see blood coming from back of head, she scream. Members of audience still laughing, at first do not notice her upsetting. When finally they realize what happen, there is panic in theater. Actors stop. Chair Traum had been sitting is empty. Black slouch hat of Traum is lying on floor in front of his seat. There is hole in it.

"As Traum leave theater, he pass gun to my father, Nathan Grinberg. He conceal gun beneath coat. Persons were in lobby during performance of play rush into theater to find out what happen. Traum leave building. Young man run up to Nathan Grinberg.

" 'Mr. Grinberg, a man has been shot!'

" 'Of course,' say Nathan, 'same man shot every night.'

" 'No,' say young man, 'I mean one of customers.'

"Young man turn around and run back into theater. Nathan Grinberg go to side door in lobby, open it, enter and shut door behind him. In middle of passageway I show you, Nathan Grinberg kneel down and remove bricks from floor. He take from hole in floor small metal box. He remove gun from coat and place it in box, then put box back into floor. He put bricks over it. Nathan stand up, brush dirt off knees and go back up passageway.

"Same night Solomon Traum, with wife and two children, are in train to Vienna."

"So Solomon Traum assassinated Rakozi," said Tanya.

"Right where we're sitting," said Robert.

Sami nodded.

"I am caretaker now of property was owned by Solomon Traum."

"What do the Ukrainians want?" Robert asked.

"Ukrainians partners with mayor, want to develop

property. They think you represent Traum family, want take property back."

"The mayor has no right to take over this property," said Tanya.

"Alexandru Rakozi, man killed by Solomon Traum, was grandfather of mayor."

"Do you know what happened to Solomon after he left Siret?" asked Robert.

"In Vienna, did many things get money support Jewish resistance in Bucovina, even rob banks. Then come Russian Revolution. Bolsheviki take over. In 1918, war end. Solomon Traum leave Austria, take family America.

"Solomon go Chicago. Work like James Cagney, Humphrey Bogart in movie. Liquor, gambling, probably even girls. Solomon write to my father, tell him come Chicago, but Nathan not want go.

"After years, Solomon become respected businessman. Send money and guns for Irgun in Palestine to fight, create Israel."

"So," said Tanya, "phantom father was gangster."

"It's understandable, isn't it?" Robert said. "Because of political repression and anti-Semitism in the

Bucovina, Solomon had been forced to take action. In Vienna, he continued to work for the cause."

"Robbing banks."

"In whatever way he could. A normal life for him was not possible."

"But he went to America. Things were different there."

"As an immigrant," said Robert, "without family or friends to help him, he used what he knew. He knew how to make money, and in the New World making money was what mattered most."

"Still now," said Sami. "Here, too."

"Buddy wrote that his father was anti-fascist, anti-communist and anti-monarchist," said Robert. "He believed in independent thought and action."

"Even here Solomon was man of action," said Sami.

"Buddy said his father betrayed no nostalgia for the old country. Solomon wanted his own children to be well educated, to be able to make choices about how they lived their lives."

"Having a choice does not always make an easier life," said Tanya.

Later, in front of the cinema, Sami shook hands with both Tanya and Robert.

"Thank you," said Robert.

"It is good story, no?" said Sami.

"It's a great story, yes," said Robert.

Tanya and Robert walked away. Sami waved at them and they waved back.

43.

A BELLBOY IN UNIFORM KNOCKED ON TANYA'S HOTEL room door. A few moments later, Tanya, dressed as she was earlier in the day, opened the door.

"Your car is waiting for you downstairs," said the bellboy.

"A car for me? There must be some mistake."

"You are Tanya Georgescu?"

"Yes."

"I was told to tell you the car is waiting."

"I didn't order any car. Why come to my room? Why not call me on the telephone?"

"I was told to escort you personally."

Tanya hesitated, then fetched her coat and left with the bellboy.

44.

TANYA WALKED OUT OF THE HOTEL AND SAW A BLACK limousine idling at the curb. A uniformed chauffeur stood on the sidewalk next to the car. The chauffeur opened the curbside rear passenger door. Tanya walked over to the car and looked inside. Tudor was seated in the backseat.

"What is this about?" Tanya asked him.

"There is a private party."

"What kind of party? Who are you?"

"My name is Tudor. You are to be a guest of Mayor Clujescu."

"I am traveling with someone, an American, Robert Botto."

"I know. I believe he is already there."

Tanya hesitated for a moment before getting into the car, then got into the backseat. The chauffeur closed the door, walked around to the driver's side and got in. The car drove away.

45.

A NEON SIGN WAS BLINKING THE WORDS "OUTKAST Klub." The limousine pulled up to the curb in front of the nightclub and stopped. The chauffeur got out, came around to the curbside passenger door and opened it. Tanya and Tudor got out of the car. Loud, hard-pounding music filled the air.

Tudor escorted Tanya into the club and led her down a stairway. They walked three or four levels below ground. As they descended, the music became even louder. Tudor led Tanya into a large, dimly lit room filled with people drinking and smoking and trying to talk over the pulsing music. On one side there was a long bar and at the opposite end of the room was an empty stage. Tudor led Tanya to a table directly in front of the stage. Tanya looked around.

"I thought you said Robert was here," said Tanya, almost shouting.

"He must be coming later," said Tudor.

"And the mayor?"

"He, too. Later."

Tudor pulled out a chair for Tanya. Reluctantly, slowly, she sat down. Tudor sat down in the chair next to her.

A masked waiter set two tall, red-colored drinks on the table in front of Tanya and Tudor. Tudor picked up his glass and extended it toward Tanya. She picked up her glass and touched it to Tudor's. They drank.

The music stopped. A fat man wearing a maroon velour dinner jacket walked onto the stage.

"And now, ladies and gentlemen," said the fat man, "it is time to present the attraction for which the Outkast Klub has become famous throughout the continent: the Five Wives of Dracula!"

The music began and five beautiful, mostly-naked young women pushed a coffin onto the stage. They began dancing around the coffin. The audience applauded wildly. Eventually, two of the dancers lifted the coffin lid. An arm appeared from within and a man made up and dressed in an elegant tuxedo with a cape like Count Dracula's sat up in the coffin. The girls surrounded him and by their movements coaxed him to leave his resting place. He climbed out and stood still. The women onstage performed as if they were dancing for him alone, to please their master.

After a few moments of this, the Master moved forward to the front of the stage, pushing aside the dancers. He looked directly at Tanya and pointed to her. The dancers left the stage and took hold of Tanya. A spotlight shined on her face. The women lifted her up and carried her onto the stage where she was

embraced by their master. The women then encircled
the couple. The Master lifted Tanya up in his arms. She
now appeared lifeless, unconscious, as he carried her to
the coffin and placed her inside it. The women closed
the lid. The Master walked offstage. The women lifted
the coffin up and carried it after him until they, too,
were offstage. The crowd applauded. Loud, pounding
music began again. Tudor, seated alone now at the table,
did not applaud. He got up and left the room.

46.

TANYA WAS ASLEEP ALONE ON A BED IN A CANDLELIT ROOM.
The door opened and the Master entered, still in cos-
tume, along with his five wives. The girls knelt down
next to the bed on all sides of her. They began caressing
her. She woke up, saw what was going on and was startled, frightened. The women undressed her. She was
powerless to resist. Tanya lay naked on the bed, the
women around her, continuing to caress her. The Master
descended over Tanya, spreading his cape.

47.

Tanya lay asleep on the bed in her hotel, naked. She woke up, dazed, woozy and saw that she was undressed. She looked around for the clothes she had been wearing the night before, but couldn't find them. Tanya stood up, went to the window and looked down at the street. A black limousine was parked at the curb. As she watched, the limousine pulled away and disappeared down the street.

48.

It was late morning. Robert was in his hotel room, packing his bag, preparing to leave. The telephone rang. Robert answered it.

"Yes?

"A woman? What's her name?

"Nicola Grigorescu?

"I don't know anyone by that name.

"Oh, yes, I do know her. I'll come down."

Robert hung up the phone.

Robert knocked on Tanya's door. He waited. There was no answer. He knocked again, but still there was no answer, so he went downstairs.

49.

Tanya was standing in the hotel lobby with Nicola Grigorescu, the music teacher. Robert walked up to them.

"Sami is dead," said Tanya.

"What happened?"

Nicola could not contain her tears.

"It seems last night he had heart attack in his office at cinema," said Tanya.

"He was supposed meet me last night my apartment," said Nicola. "It become very late but Sami not arrive. I do not have telephone. I go to cinema, find Sami dead. I call police. This morning Ukrainian men come, say they now own cinema and synagogue buildings. Tell me before Sami die, he sell properties to them."

"This doesn't make sense," said Robert.

"Perhaps you can help me," Nicola said to Tanya. "Ukrainian men tell me I have to leave. They put lock on door."

Nicola began to cry again.

50.

TANYA AND ROBERT STOOD IN FRONT OF THE MAYOR'S desk in his office, behind which Mayor Clujescu was seated.

"Sami Grinberg?" said the mayor. "Oh yes, the old man who runs the cinema. He's also the caretaker of the old synagogue, isn't he? What about him?"

"He is dead," said Tanya. "He may have been killed."

"For what reason? He could not have very much money, although these Jews are thrifty. They often have more than they let on."

"Two Ukrainian men have been trying to acquire the properties that Sami holds the deeds to," said Robert.

"What is your relation to Sami Grinberg?" the mayor asked Robert.

"He was helping me with research for a book I'm writing."

"We were with Sami Grinberg yesterday," said Tanya. "He told us he had no intention of selling these properties."

"Perhaps he changed his mind," said Clujescu. "He may have received a better offer than he expected."

Tanya stared at the mayor and then said, "If you are

unwilling to assist us in this matter, I will have to go to another authority."

"These kinds of things happen when foreigners come into the country. Our people are simple, they are easily taken advantage of."

"Listen, Clujescu, don't fuck with me," said Tanya. "I know you're in bed with the Ukrainians. I am going to find out what really happened to Sami Grinberg."

"I do not know where you get your information nor what your interest in the situation is."

"It is enough for you to know that I am interested."

She then turned to Robert and said, "We must return to Suceava. There are people there who will help us."

"Oh, Mademoiselle Georgescu," said the mayor, "I am sorry I was late for the party. By the time I arrived, you had already left."

Robert looked at Tanya. She stared at the mayor, then left the office, followed by Robert.

51.

TANYA WAS DRIVING IN HER CAR AT NIGHT; ROBERT WAS in the passenger seat. The road was dark and treacherous.

Suddenly, another car appeared driving close behind them and flashed its headlights. Tanya looked in the rearview mirror and Robert turned in his seat to look at the car following them. All they could discern were two rather large silhouettes in the front seat.

Tanya sped up, trying to put more distance between her car and theirs, but the mystery car kept up with her. Tanya turned off the main road, hoping the mystery car would not follow, but it did.

The mystery car chased them through the mountains, which became increasingly perilous as Tanya sped around many hairpin turns. Finally, the mystery car failed to negotiate a sharp curve and drove off a cliff. Tanya pulled her car to the side of the road and stopped. She was exhausted and collapsed in tears in Robert's arms.

52.

ON THE MOUNTAIN ROAD THERE WAS A BAR PATRONIZED mostly by Hungarian woodsmen, many of whom appeared to be drunk. It was very late. Tanya and Robert entered, obviously shaken by the previous events. The bar patrons stared at Tanya and Robert.

Tanya whispered to Robert, "This is Magyar bar. They are Hungarians who do not consider themselves part of Romania. I do not want to speak Romanian to them. You speak in English, it will be better. *American* English."

Robert approached the bartender.

"Hello, we're lost. We're trying to get to Suceava, but we must have taken the wrong road. Can you tell us how to get there?"

"Yes, it is not difficult," said the bartender. "Would you like something to drink?"

"Yes, thank you. Coffee would be fine."

An older, drunken woodsman, holding an empty glass in one hand and an axe in the other, came up to Robert and said in Hungarian, "You are from Russia?"

Robert looked at the bartender and asked him, "Can you tell me what he's saying?"

The bartender served coffee to Tanya and Robert.

"He asks if you are from Russia."

"Tell him I'm from California," said Robert.

The bartender leaned toward the drunken woodsman and said in Hungarian, "He says he's from California."

The drunken woodsman said to Robert, in Hungarian, "Do they get drunk in California?"

Robert looked at the bartender.

"I think he wants you to buy him a drink," said the bartender.

Robert took money from his pocket and placed it on the bar.

"I'll be glad to."

The drunken woodsman put his glass down on the bar, picked up Robert's money and handed it back to him. The drunken woodsman then took money from his own pocket, put it on the bar and said to the bartender, in Hungarian, "*I* want to buy *them* a drink."

"I am wrong," said the bartender to Robert. "He says he wants to buy you and your lady a drink."

"Thank you," Robert said to the drunken woodsman. "We could probably use one."

The bartender took down two glasses and removed a bottle from a shelf and poured drinks for Robert and Tanya.

"*Tokaji.* Hungarian wine. Very good."

Then the bartender poured from the bottle into the drunken woodsman's glass. The three of them clinked their glasses together.

"*Ege'sze'ge're!*" said the drunken woodsman.

They drank.

53.

TANYA AND ROBERT LAY IN BED IN TANYA'S APARTMENT in Suceava, half asleep. It was late night or early morning. They were naked under the covers. Robert held her tightly to him and spoke softly into her ear.

"Tanya, I have to ask you, are you *Securitate?*"

"It does not really matter, does it?"

She kissed him. They began to make love.

Robert woke up alone in Tanya's bed. On the pillow next to him was a note. Robert read it, put it down and got out of bed.

54.

ROBERT ENTERED TANYA'S OFFICE AT CITY HALL. TANYA was seated behind a desk. He walked over and stood on the opposite side of the desk from her. She stood up.

"We must return to Siret," she said.

"Is this room bugged?" asked Robert.

"Bug?"

He leaned toward her and said softly, "Can anyone hear what I'm saying?"

"I can."

"May I kiss you?"

"Can you wait?"

"I'd rather not."

"Then do not."

"Do not kiss or do not wait?"

Tanya leaned forward and kissed him.

"When do we leave?" asked Robert.

"Now."

55.

"Mayor Clujescu says Sami did make deal with Ukrainians," said Tanya, as she drove, "but it is no good because they were killed in automobile accident before they could make payment. In will, Sami leave properties to music teacher, Nicola Grigorescu."

"She was his mistress," said Robert.

"Probably, yes."

"Tanya, just before we left Clujescu's office, he mentioned missing you at a party."

"I do not remember."

She began driving faster.

"Slow down," said Robert, "these roads can be dangerous."

56.

TANYA, ROBERT AND NICOLA WERE IN THE SYNAGOGUE. Nicola wrote "SAMI GRINBERG" on the wall under the name of his father, Nathan Grinberg.

Robert looked again at the name "SOLOMON TRAUM." He reached out and touched it with the fingers of his right hand. "For Buddy," he said.

57.

THE WEATHER WAS SPRING-LIKE, THE SUN WAS SHINING. A postman approached the cinema, opened the door and went in. Standing in the lobby was Nicola Grigorescu. The postman handed her a package and left. Nicola opened it and took out a book.

The title of the book was *Beautiful Phantoms: A Biography of Rudolph Traum* by Robert Botto.

Nicola opened the book to the title page, which Robert had signed. Above his signature, he had written,

"See the dedication—Narok!" Nicola turned to the dedication page, which read, "This book is dedicated to the memory of Sami Grinberg."

The doors of the theater opened as people entered. Inside the theater, projected on the screen, was an old black-and-white film showing a man and a woman walking arm in arm as snow fell. A horse and carriage followed by an early-model car passed them on the street. The snowfall increased, filling the screen with twirling, white flakes.

Paloma gave it

up to me in

the balcony

man they can't

tear down

my memory

The God of Birds

࿊࿊࿊࿊࿊࿊࿊࿊࿊࿊

San Francisco

WHILE ROY WAS WAITING TO GET A HAIRCUT AT DUKE'S Barber Shop, Roy was reading an article in a hunting and fishing magazine about a man in Northern Asia who hunted wolves with only a golden eagle as a weapon. This man rode a horse, holding on one arm a four-foot-long golden eagle around the shore of a mountain lake in a country next to China from November to March looking for prey. Beginning each day before dawn, the eagle master, called a berkutchi, cloaked in a black velvet robe from neck to ankle to protect him from fierce mountain winds, rode out alone with his huge bird. The berkutchi scoffed at those who practiced falconry, said the article in the magazine, deriding it as a sport for children and cowards.

"Eagles are the most magnificent of hunting beasts," said the master. "My eagle has killed many large-horned ibex by shoving them off cliffs. He would fight a man if I commanded him to do so."

The berkutchi's eagle, who was never given a name, had been with him for more than thirty years. He had students, the article said, whom the berkutchi instructed in the ways to capture and train eagles.

"I can only show them how it is done," said the master, "but I would never give away the real secrets. These secrets a man must learn by himself, or he will not become a successful hunter. A man is only a man, but the eagle is the god of birds."

"Roy!" Duke the barber shouted. "Didn't ya hear me? You're next!"

Roy closed the magazine and put it back on the card table in the waiting area.

When he was in the chair, Duke asked him, "Find somethin' interestin' inna magazine, kid?"

"Yes, an article about a guy in the mountains of Asia who hunts wolves on horseback with an eagle."

"How old are you now, Roy?"

"Almost twelve."

"Think you could do that?" Duke asked, as he clipped. "Learn how to hunt with a bird?"

Duke was in his mid-forties, mostly bald, with a three-day beard. Roy had never seen Duke clean shaven, even though he was a barber. His shop had three chairs but only one other man worked with him, a Puerto Rican named Alfredito. Alfredito was missing the last three fingers of his right hand, the one in which he held the scissors. When Roy asked him how he'd lost them, Alfredito said a donkey had bitten them off when he was a boy back in Bayamon. Roy never allowed Alfredito to cut his hair anymore because Alfredito always nicked him. He got his hair cut on Thursdays now, which was Alfredito's day off. Duke told Roy that Alfredito worked Thursdays for his brother, Ramon, who had a tailor shop over by Union Square. Roy wondered if Alfredito could sew better than he could cut hair with only one finger on his right hand.

"I don't know," Roy answered. "Maybe if I grew up there and had a good berkutchi."

"Berkutchi? What's that?"

"An eagle master. The one in the magazine said the eagle is the god of birds."

The door to the shop opened and an old man wearing a gray fedora came in.

"Mr. Majewski, hello," said Duke. "Have a seat, I'll be right with you."

Mr. Majewski stared at Alfredito's empty chair and said, "So where is the Puerto Rican boy?"

"It's Thursday, Mr. Majewski. Alfredito don't work for me on Thursdays."

"He works tomorrow?" asked Mr. Majewski.

"Yeah, he'll be here."

"I'll come tomorrow," Majewski said, and walked out.

"You want it short today, Roy?"

"Leave it long in the back, Duke. I don't like my neck to feel scratchy."

"I used to shoot birds when I was a boy," said Duke, "up in the Delta."

As he was walking home from the barber shop, a sudden brisk wind caused Roy to put up the collar of his leather jacket. Then it began to rain. Roy walked faster, imagining how terrible the weather could get during the winter months in the mountains of rural

Asia. Even a four-foot-long golden eagle must sometimes have a difficult time flying against a cold, hard
wind hurtling out of the Caucasus, Roy thought, when
he saw a gray hat being blown past him down the
middle of Dolores Street. He did not stop to see if it
was Mr. Majewski's fedora.

The chicken his name

was Octavio

                    he would

        follow me around

    Octavio ate corn

            from the palm

            of my hand

    he never pecked me

        with his beak

            my cousin Rodrigo

                murdered him

        with a hatchet

                put Octavio's head

        on my pillow

                    I was seven

                        years old

            I still have

                that pillow

            with Octavio's blood

                        on it

Dancing with Fidel

ぬぬぬぬぬぬぬぬぬぬぬ

Havana

THINGS WERE NOT WORKING OUT THE WAY MARY HAD thought they would. The weather was fine, warm with the tradewinds to keep the temperature bearable, about what she had expected to experience in Miami Beach—*sultry,* Mary's best friend Donna back in Dorchester had called it after her honeymoon there the year before. Mary loved the sound of that word, 'sultry'; it was a real sexy word, she thought. The hotel was nice, too, clean and elegant without being ostentatious like some of the others she'd seen strung along the beach, false pearls whose gaudy facades faded day by day under pressure from the relentless sun and salty sea air.

No, the tropical setting was satisfactory; it was Walter Turner, her husband of three days, who was not.

Mary Keaton Turner sat in a beach chair next to the Spearfish Hotel swimming pool wearing a yellow two-piece swimsuit and cat's-eye sunglasses. She was smoking a cigarette, watching Walter breaststroke his way the length of the pool. He was a good swimmer, Mary realized. She, on the other hand, could not swim a stroke. That she could do no better than dog paddle had not bothered her until now; seeing even small children splash their way from one end of the gigantic pool to the other made her feel suddenly inadequate, embarrassed to be so natatorily inept at the age of twenty-three. Walter, who was twenty-eight, had learned the Australian crawl, he said, when he was seven years old.

Walter was a good person, Mary knew, kind and generous, better-than-average-looking, and he already earned more than most men in middle-management positions. Mary had examined the statistics on salaries for the previous year, 1959, in *Fortune* magazine, when she was having her hair lightened the day before the wedding, and she felt confident that Walter had a bright financial future. Everyone, friends and family, agreed that he was an excellent catch. Perhaps he was, but Mary found him, in a word, dull. He had made love to her only once in their three-day-old union and he insisted on going to sleep no later than ten or ten-thirty at night. Swimming, sunning and shopping for trinkets tired him out, Walter told Mary. If she wanted to stay up, that was all right with him, but he was a man who knew—and was not discomforted by—his limitations. So far, Mary had gone to bed when Walter had, but tonight, she decided, would be different.

After dinner on the hotel verandah, Mary and Walter went to the Spearfish cocktail bar and lounge with another newlywed couple they had met poolside that afternoon. Eddie and Diana Rogers were from Cincinnati; he was thirty-one, she twenty-five. They seemed to Mary an amiable but unremarkable pair—Eddie was a certified public accountant, Diana a secretary at a law office—but Mary craved company other than Walter, so when she spotted them dining on the verandah as well, she went over and suggested they rendezvous in the bar afterwards.

As they sat at a table and talked, all four having ordered

strawberry daiquiris at Diana's insistence—"You won't believe how divine they make you feel!"—Mary contemplated her dilemma. Walter was simply the wrong guy for her, she decided. A nice guy, but not the man with whom she could now envision herself spending the remainder of her life. Why she had not realized this before was not really so difficult to understand: While technically not a virgin due to a lone episode when she was seventeen, Mary had not slept with Walter until their wedding night; unsurprisingly, it had not been a rousing (she almost giggled at her thought of the word) success, though she believed that was bound to improve. There were so many details to attend to before the wedding, so many distractions, that any doubts about the wisdom of her decision to wed Walter were relegated to a far remove of Mary's mind; she simply could not get to them in time, much to her regret. What to do? Mary pondered, as Walter, Eddie and Diana made small talk. Tomorrow, Mary decided, she would call her mother in Dorchester and feel her out about it, though her mother, Mary knew, would almost certainly advise her to give Walter a chance; after all, he was new at this, too.

At precisely nine forty-five, Mary's husband told

the others that he was bushed and was going upstairs to bed.

"All of that swimming took a lot out of me today," he said.

Walter stood up and looked at Mary, a relaxed smile on his face.

"But you haven't finished your daiquiri," said Diana Rogers.

"I'll finish it," Mary said. "Mine's kaput. You won't mind if I stay a little while longer with Eddie and Diana, do you, Walter?"

"Of course not," he answered. "Stay as long as you like."

After Walter left, Diana began talking about show dogs, about which Mary knew nothing. Diana and Eddie had a prize border collie that in the past two years had won four blue ribbons.

"We're thinking of taking Clipper to the national competition at Madison Square Garden next year," Diana told her.

"May I join you?"

Mary and the Rogers couple looked up to see a well-groomed man of about forty standing next to their table. His thick black hair was slicked straight back; he was wearing what appeared to be a diamond stickpin in the lapel of his double-breasted blue suit, as well as a diamond pinky ring on his left hand.

"I'm by myself here, and I'll be happy to buy you a new round of fresh drinks."

Eddie gestured to the chair vacated by Walter.

"Please yourself," he said.

"Thank you," said the man, and sat down.

He signalled to a waiter, who came over immediately.

"Fresh drinks, all around, Sidney," he said. "What are you having?" he asked the others.

"Strawberry daiquiris," said Diana.

"Beautiful. Three fresh daiquiris, Sidney, and my usual. A double."

Sidney nodded and went away.

"What is your 'usual,' Mr . . ." asked Eddie.

"Victor. Vic Victor."

Eddie and Diana introduced themselves.

"Where you from?" Vic Victor asked.

"Cincinnati," said Diana.

"New York," said Mary.

"Where New York?" Vic Victor asked her.

"Dorchester County."

"I know Dorchester," Vic said.

"Yourself?" asked Eddie.

"Here and there," said Vic. "Here now."

Diana laughed and said, " 'There' later."

"No," said Vic, " 'there' before, 'where' later." He laughed, punctuating it with a throaty sound that Mary could identify only as *"Mm-mm-ff."*

Sidney returned and placed three daiquiris and a double scotch on the rocks on the table.

"Fresh drinks," said Vic, and handed a folded bill to Sidney, who took it and went away again. Vic lifted his glass. "Bombs away," he said.

After they had all taken a sip of their drinks, Mary said, "May I ask, Mr. Victor, what it is that you're doing here? I don't mean to be rude."

"Rude? A pretty girl like you?" said Vic. "New York girl? Not a chance. Here I don't do much."

The four of them chatted and drank for about an hour, then Vic said, "Eddie, do you like to gamble? Cards, dice, roulette?"

"I was in Vegas once," Eddie said.

"Did you like it?"

"I did," said Eddie. "I liked playing craps."

"Listen,"Vic said,"I got a private plane chartered to go to Havana tonight, in"—he looked at his gold-banded watch—"forty minutes. It takes a half-hour to get there, thirty minutes. Come with me, why doncha? You ever been to Cuba? Great casinos. I pay the pilot. We'll be back here in a few hours."

Diana laughed. "Fly to Havana now?"

"Yeah, sure," said Vic. "Why not?"

Eddie looked at his wife. "What do you think, hon'?" he asked.

"I'll go if Mary goes."

They looked at Mary. She took a sip of her fresh daiquiri. She thought of Walter, asleep upstairs in their room.

"Why not?" she said.

In the taxi on the way to the airport Mary was seized by a sudden fear that what she was doing was crazy. She didn't really know any of these people, especially Vic Victor. He might be a gangster, she thought, not merely a gambler. Cuba was another country, one whose government had recently been overthrown. She had heard Cuba referred to as the whorehouse of the Caribbean. The new regime had vowed to change that, to properly educate, house and feed everyone on the island. Mary had no idea what to expect. Eddie and Diana were giddy with excitement.

At Vic's direction, the taxi took them right onto the runway of a small airport where an eight-passenger plane awaited their arrival. Mary and the Rogers couple followed Vic Victor onto the plane, which started up immediately and began taxiing down the runway as soon as Vic secured the door. He went forward and spoke briefly to the pilot, then sat down in a seat across the aisle from Mary.

"That's Hal, folks," he said. The pilot waved one of his hands at them without turning around. "We're old pals," Vic told them. Then he shouted at Hal, "We're old friends, aren't we, Hal?"

Hal signalled a thumbs-up, keeping his eyes straight ahead. The passengers buckled up and the plane took off.

Once they were airborne, Vic opened an ice chest and offered the others a cold beer. Mary, Eddie and Diana each took one. Vic did not, however, and Eddie said to him, "You're not drinking?"

Vic shook his head. "Can't," he said. "If something happened to Hal—heart attack, brain aneurysm—I'd have to take over. Gotta keep my mind clear, just in case."

"You can fly?" asked Diana.

Vic nodded.

"Eighty-one missions in Korea," he said. "Two confirmed kills, one disputed. I know I nailed that third Russki, though. But don't worry, Hal has the constitution of a lizard. Don't you, Hal?" Vic shouted at him. "I told these people you've got the constitution of a lizard."

Hal nodded, then again gave a thumbs-up without turning around.

"Only problem with Hal," said Vic, "is that one of his eyes got poked out in a bar fight six years ago. Seminole Indian used a pool cue on him. Can't tell the glass eye from the real one. He flies a plane good as ever, though. Just once in a while he miscalculates slightly on the landing. Almost skidded us into a lake full of alligators last May. Hey, Hal," Vic shouted, "which one of your eyes is the glass one?"

Hal shot Vic a middle finger, and Vic cracked up.

"Just a joke, folks," he said. "My old pal Hal has the eyesight of an eagle. Drink up, we're almost there."

Hal landed the plane expertly, with hardly a bounce, at the Havana airport, taxied for a few minutes and stopped in front of a terminal. After landing, he began writing on a piece of paper attached to a clipboard. Vic opened the door, lowered the boarding steps and exited first.

"Thanks, Hal," Eddie said, "see you on the way back to Miami."

Hal waved his pencil but did not turn around.

Vic guided his charges toward customs, and told them, "Don't say a word, just follow me."

At customs, Vic produced a permit or document of some kind—neither Mary nor the Rogers couple could see what it was—and he and the others were waved through without delay. The Cuban official merely nodded at Vic as he passed by, and hardly seemed to notice Eddie, Diana or Mary. The four of them climbed into a Cadillac taxi and sped away from the airport.

"We're going to El Gallo," Vic announced, "the best casino and dance club in Cuba. Trust me."

"We don't have a choice but to trust you, do we, Mr. Victor?" asked Mary.

"Of course, you do, Mary," he said. "You always have a choice. It's just that sometimes it's better to let things happen."

In ten minutes they arrived at El Gallo. In three

minutes more they were inside the club and being led to a table. There was a stage on which a twenty-piece orchestra was performing, and a dance floor crowded with couples. Most of the tables in the club were occupied. The music was loud and upbeat and the patrons were talking, laughing, drinking and dancing in as lively a manner as Mary had ever seen.

"The casino is in another room," Vic said to Eddie, as the four of them sat down.

Without their having ordered, tall rum drinks with enormous pieces of fruit draped over the sides of the glasses were placed in front of them. The music was so loud that Mary could barely hear a word anybody said, so she sipped her drink, which was terribly sweet but strong, and watched the dancers. After several minutes, Eddie said something to Diana and he and Vic left the table together. Diana scooted her chair close to Mary's and said, "They're going to gamble. Do you want to go with them?"

Mary shook her head.

"I'm fine here," she said.

Diana and Mary sipped their drinks and enjoyed the spectacle. After a few more minutes, Diana said to

Mary, "Do you see those men over there? The ones wearing battle fatigues."

She motioned toward them with her head. Mary looked in the direction Diana indicated and saw four bearded men in military uniforms, smoking cigars.

"Yes," said Mary.

"Well," said Diana, "the one on the left, wearing a hat, has been staring at you since we sat down. I think he likes you."

At that moment, the man stood up and walked over to their table. He took off his hat and looked directly at Mary.

"Would you do me the honor of dancing with me?" he asked her.

The man was very tall and lean, with a long, thin reddish-brown beard. Before Mary could say anything, he had taken her by the hand and led her onto the dance floor. The tune was a mambo and Mary did her best to keep up. Her partner, she quickly realized, was not a very much better dancer than she, so they managed to accommodate each other without one of them being embarrassed by their own lack of expertise. Halfway through the number, Mary began to relax and enjoy dancing with this man, who smiled at her often, revealing severely tobacco-stained teeth. She liked his dark brown eyes, which were soft and warm and very bright.

Out of the corner of her right eye, Mary saw Vic Victor moving quickly toward her. When he was within ten feet, Vic withdrew a revolver from one of his coat pockets, pointed it at her dance partner and pulled the trigger. Just as he did so, before she could react, someone knocked his gun hand up and deflected the bullet harmlessly into the ceiling. Chaos, of course, ensued, and the next thing Mary knew, she was being half-carried out of the club and shoved into the backseat of a car. Diana and Eddie Rogers soon joined her in the backseat, and as soon as they were safely inside, the door closed and the car drove off. Mary did not know who was driving or where they were going. Diana had collapsed in tears and Eddie was trembling visibly. Mary looked into the front seat and saw that a black man wearing green army fatigues was at the wheel. In the passenger seat was another of the bearded men who had been seated at the table with her dance partner.

The car sped rapidly through the night and soon Mary realized they were approaching the airfield where their plane had landed. Then she saw the plane. The car drove up to it and stopped. The bearded man got out and opened a rear door. Eddie disembarked first, followed by his wife and then Mary. The bearded man led them to the plane and motioned for them to board, which they did. As Mary took a seat, the engine turned over. She saw that Hal was at the controls. The door slammed shut and the plane began taxiing down the runway. It took off. Nobody said a word during the flight.

The plane landed in Miami thirty minutes later. A black Chrysler sedan was waiting. Eddie, Diana and Mary got in and were driven by a brown-skinned man to the Spearfish Hotel. Again, nobody spoke.

In the lobby of the hotel, Eddie said to Mary, "I think it would be better if we didn't see each other again." Then he and Diana walked quickly away.

Mary looked at the clock above the registration desk. It was four-thirty in the morning.

She took the elevator to her floor, got off and went to her room. Walter was asleep, snoring softly. Mary took her suitcase from the closet, opened it and began to pack her clothes.

I got almost

   all the way now

    through my life

           and I never hated

       another person

  no matter what

         anyone done

     How many people

    you know

could say this

         without it

    be a lie?

The Sculptor's Son

ഗ്രഗ്രഗ്രഗ്രഗ്രഗ്ര

Paris

SEVERAL YEARS AGO, WHEN I WAS SUFFERING THE aftermath of divorce from my first wife, I fled to Paris in an attempt to restore myself. At a dinner party one night while I was there, I met a young doctor who told me an interesting story. Didier was several years younger than I, charming and cheerful. Just talking with him buoyed my spirits. He asked me what I was doing in France and after I'd told him, he smiled and said that his father seemed to have an answer for dealing with failed or passé relationships. I responded that I was eager to hear about it.

Didier's father, he told me, had been married six or seven times, Didier was not sure, and had had almost that many live-in mistresses. Didier's mother had been the second wife. There were eleven children in all, never more than one with each wife or mistress. Didier's father owned a large house outside Paris, a house that had steadily grown larger and more compartmentalized over the years. The reason for this expansion was a result of Didier's father's solution.

Each time his father decided that a marital or pseudo-marital situation had deteriorated irreparably, Didier explained, he began building a partition within the house or an addition to it, creating new living quarters for himself. He never asked his lame-duck partner to leave or even to divorce; he just stopped arguing, cut himself off from her and created another space to occupy. Some of the women became upset, Didier said, and immediately or eventually moved away; others, for various reasons, particularly those with children, stayed on. Didier's father made no attempt to explain his actions; soon the pattern became obvious, then expected.

How many women still lived in his father's house? I asked Didier. Nine, he answered, including his father's present wife, who was pregnant. Do the women get along? I wanted to know. Some do, some don't, said Didier. It's like a small town. For the sake of the children, of whom there are six—soon to be seven—in residence, he said, the women make an effort to be decent to one another. Are the estranged wives and former mistresses allowed to bring other men to the house? Of course, they can, replied Didier, they can do whatever they like; except the men cannot live at the house, only visit. My father insists, quite reasonably, I think, that his financial responsibility is to the women and his children only. If one of the women enters into a domestic relationship with a man, or becomes pregnant by a man other than my father, she is made to leave. His father, Didier assured me, was not an ungenerous man; each woman was always amply provided for.

I asked Didier what his father's profession was. He's a sculptor, Didier said, quite a successful one. But the family has been wealthy for generations; they own banks in Switzerland and America.

His father reminded me in a way of another artist, I said, Picasso, who every seven years or so supposedly moved out of an apartment or house and left everything behind just as it was, perhaps never to return. Unlike Didier's father, however, Picasso did not allow his women to remain.

And what about you? I asked Didier. Have you adopted your father's method? He laughed and said, No, at least not yet. In fact, Didier told me, he and his fiancée had recently moved into his father's house. His girlfriend was amused by the arrangement, this seraglio. Thus far, she was getting along well with everyone. With your father, too? I asked. At this, the young doctor favored me with a half-smile and said, My father told me that she resembles his fourth wife, Claire, a woman I barely knew and who stayed with him only a short time, the briefest of all, before leaving. My father never saw Claire again. Anyway, that's the name by which my father refers to my fiancée when talking to me. Does he call her Claire when addressing her directly? I asked. Oh, no, Didier said, my father never speaks to her, just as he never speaks to any of his exes. But she's your intended, I said, your wife-to-be, not a former one of his. I know, said the sculptor's son, but when he sees her he thinks of Claire. I understand him, and my girlfriend doesn't seem to mind.

Somewhere up

there

they found

her

body

man

I heard

it

was pretty

fucked

up

Wanted Man

Florida

THE SUMMER I WAS THIRTEEN YEARS OLD I WORKED IN Cocoa Beach, Florida, building roads and houses for my uncle's construction company. One afternoon when we were paving a street in one hundred and five degree heat, a police car pulled up to the site, stopped, and two cops got out, guns drawn. They moved swiftly toward the steam roller, which was being operated by Boo Ruffert, a former Georgia sheriff. The cops proceeded without a word and grabbed Boo, dragging him down from his perch atop the steamroller. I was shoveling lime rock off of a curb directly across from the action, and I watched the cops handcuff Ruffert and begin double-timing him toward their beige and white. Jake Farkas, who had been sweeping behind Boo, jumped up onto the steamroller and shut it down before the machine went out of control and careened off the road. My uncle came running out of the trailer he used as an office and intercepted the policemen before they locked Boo Ruffert into the patrol car.

"Wait!" my uncle shouted at the cops. "What are you doing with him?"

"This man is wanted on a charge of child molestation in Georgia," said one of them. "We have a warrant for his arrest."

"Want to see it?" asked the other cop. He was holding the nose of his revolver against Ruffert's right temple.

"Listen," said my uncle, "Boo here is my best heavy equipment operator. He's almost finished with this street."

My uncle pulled out a roll of bills from one of his trouser pockets.

"Let me buy you fellows some lunch. Ruffert won't go anywhere, I'll keep an eye on him. You boys have something to eat while he finishes up here."

He held two fifties out toward them. "How about it?"

The cops looked at the money in my uncle's hand, then stuffed Ruffert into the backseat.

"Sorry," said one, "you'll have to get yourself another man. This one's headed to the hoosegow."

I had walked over and stood watching and listening to this exchange. I looked at Ruffert through the left-side rear window. Boo grinned at me, exposing several brown teeth, and winked his right eye, the one with the heart-shaped blood spot on the lower outside corner of the white. I guessed Boo's age to be about forty. Jake Farkas came up and stood next to me. Jake always had the stub of a dead Indian, as he called cigars, in his mouth, usually a crook, and three or four days' worth of whiskers on his face. He was in his early thirties but had already fathered, he told me, approximately thirteen children.

"You think you can ride her down the rest of the way?" my uncle asked Jake.

"Sure thing," Jake said.

My uncle turned and walked back to the trailer.

"Did you know about Boo?" I asked. "That he was a wanted man?"

Jake chuckled and said, "My dear old mama used to say it's always good to be wanted, but I'm older now and I know that my dear old mama weren't always right."

Jake strode to the steamroller, hopped up into the

seat and cranked it over. I went back to shoveling lime rock.

That evening, after my uncle dropped me off at a local movie theater while he went off to play cards, a bizarre incident occurred. I figured he was going to see a woman and that he knew I knew but seeing as how he had a wife in Miami, I assumed he thought it prudent not to tell me any more than he had to. I was not particularly fond of my aunt; my uncle knew this and most probably also knew I would never have betrayed his confidence had he chosen to tell me the truth, but this way neither of us had to compromise ourselves.

The movie was *Zulu,* which depicted red-jacketed, heavily armed British soldiers in South Africa battling against Shaka's spear-throwing warriors. The theater was segregated; white patrons were seated downstairs and black patrons were seated in the balcony. This was in 1964, so some small progress had been made regarding racial equality in Florida in that both whites and blacks were at least allowed to be in the movie theater together.

The redcoats were vastly outnumbered by the Zulus, but their highly disciplined British square defense—one line kneeling and firing as the line behind them stood and cleaned and reloaded their rifles—kept the natives at bay. The outcome, however, was inevitable; at some point the Zulus would overwhelm them. As the battle raged, there came from the balcony increasing shouts of exhortation directed at the Zulus, which incited equally fervent vocalizing by the white members of the audience below. The din inside the theater grew louder and more and more heated, practically drowning out the soundtrack of the picture.

Suddenly, the lights in the theater came on and the film stopped. The cinema manager jumped up onstage and stood in front of the screen. He was a large, mostly bald, clean-shaven white man wearing a baggy green suit. He held a lit cigarette between the second and third fingers of his right hand, the one he used to gesticulate and point toward the balcony. The crowd was silent.

"Listen up!" he shouted. "Any further ruckus and I'm throwin' all you niggers out of here!"

The manager kept his two cigarette fingers pointed at the balcony section for at least twenty seconds longer; then he put them to his mouth, took a long drag on the cigarette, exhaled smoke so that it curlicued slowly away from him and vanished in the lights, and dropped the butt to the floor where he ground it out with his right shoe. He did not lower his eyes from the cheap seats until he jumped down from the stage and unhurriedly proceeded up the center aisle and out into the lobby. The sound of the doors swinging shut was the only noise in the theater until the house lights blinked out and the projector resumed rolling.

The film ended with Shaka's Zulus acknowledging the bravery and ingenuity of the British regulars by saluting them and deciding against slaughtering them wholesale, thereby emerging victorious by having made the grandest and noblest heroic gesture possible before disappearing over a distant rise. I waited until almost every other patron had left the theater before I did. There was no trouble outside. The manager stood in front of the ticket booth, smoking. Up close, I could see several dark stains on the jacket and pants of his suit.

My uncle was parked in front of the theater. I climbed into his white Cadillac convertible and he drove away.

"How was the show?" he asked.

"Good," I said, "there was lots of fighting. Did you win?"

"Win?"

"Yeah, at the poker game."

"A little," said my uncle. "I always win a little."

We drove for a while without saying anything, then I asked, "What do you think will happen to Boo?"

"He'll do some hard time, I'm sure," my uncle said. "It's a bad business, messing with children."

"Was it a boy or a girl that he messed with?"

"A girl."

"How old was she?"

"Jake told me she was ten."

"How does he know?"

"What difference does it make? Ruffert was a wanted man, you won't ever see him again. Tell me more about the movie."

That old DelRay

             he come stormin' out

     wavin' that

          switchblade

        Buddy coldcocked

  him with a tire iron

      that's his head

              lyin'

        over in the bush

       red ants

            ate out

        the eyeballs

Murder at the Swordfish Club

ഔഔഔഔഔഔഔഔഔഔഔ

New Zealand

1.

RUSSELL IS A QUIET TOWN. OTHER THAN THE SIX WEEKS or so surrounding Christmas when the beautiful people, as Moss Hawks calls them, descend on the place, it's a peaceful fishing village of approximately six hundred residents. Virtually everyone knows everyone else. The town is located on a peninsula in the Bay of Islands, Northland, New Zealand, and is accessible by ferryboat from Paihia or Opua, or by road through a dense forest, an arduous drive in the best of circumstances, about four and a half hours north from Auckland, the largest city in the country. Mount Cook

Airlines flies to Kerikeri, about twenty minutes by car from Paihia; and the ferry crossing takes a quarter of an hour, so it's a rather remote place. Interestingly enough, Russell—or as it was then known, Kororareka—was the first capital of New Zealand.

The Bay of Islands Swordfish Club was founded in 1918, and was originally named the Bay of Islands Kingfish Club. In 1924, the name was altered to the B. of I. Swordfish and Mako Shark Club, and over the years shortened to its present title. Zane Grey, the American writer of western shoot-'em-ups such as *Riders of the Purple Sage,* traveled to the Bay of Islands in 1926 and established a fishing camp at Otehei Bay, near Russell. He hung out at the Swordfish Club and became famous in New Zealand for introducing new methods of deep-sea fishing to the area, most prominently the apparatus of a reel mounted on top of a rod instead of underneath, thus producing less wear and tear on the line. Grey wrote in his book, *Tales of the Angler's Eldorado:* "It is impossible to fight a great game fish with reel and guides underneath the rod. I mean *stop* him and *fight* him . . . Reel and guides must be on top, because if they are not . . . the angler cannot *pull* with all his might." Grey also advocated use of a single hook in place of the three hooks New Zealanders then employed. In an article in the New Zealand *Herald,* Zane Grey said, "It is no trick and no sport to catch a fish on a great big murderous triple hook."

The locals found Grey to be an arrogant, often nasty, self-important fellow, and a womanizer to boot. For his part, the western novelist didn't have too much good to say about the Bay of Islanders. Neither did he care for the Tahitians—other than the women, whose long hair he contrasted favorably to the fashion of the American women of the 1920s who chopped their hair off short and had "bristly necks"—he encountered on his voyage through the South Pacific. His book, *Tales,* praised the fishing in the Bay of Islands, but in it he excoriated the citizens for what he perceived as their shortcomings and reluctance to adopt his methods. Grey did much to publicize the place, however, and so he is mentioned prominently in local lore.

The Swordfish Club, located on the Strand, directly on the waterfront near the wharf, is the central institution of the town. The sixteen original members hailed not only from Russell but also Wellington, Waihaha,

Whangarei and Auckland. Their professions included a Police Constable (the only policeman in Russell—there is *still* only one), Harbour Master, Launch Proprietor, Launch Driver, Farmer, Contractor, Postmaster, Schoolmaster, Shipping Agent, Boardinghouse Keeper, University Lecturer and one Married Woman. A representative gathering of solid citizens. The club was duly incorporated under the New Zealand Societies Act of 1908, and noted as the initial entry in its annals that the first recorded catch of a swordfish was landed by a Mr. Campbell in February 1913. Mr. Campbell's fish weighed 220 pounds. In the visitors recording book for 1929-30, the first kept by the club, anglers signed in from Kenya Colony, London, Chicago, New York, Germany, Singapore, Sydney, Ceylon, Boston and Scotland. Zane Grey had put the Bay of Islands on the Big Game Fishing Map as the Angler's Eldorado.

At nine-thirty on the morning of Sunday, May 1, 1988, Hunt Terry, the secretary of the Bay of Islands Swordfish Club, discovered on the front porch of the upstairs bar the dead body of Billy Boy Reynolds, a local fisherman and charter boat captain who was a native of Russell. Mr. Reynolds, who was a Maori, was forty-seven years old at the time someone put a gun to his right temple and blew his brains onto The Strand. This, Hunt Terry told Liam Jones, the town policeman, was the first recorded murder in the seventy-year history of the Swordfish Club.

2.

ACCORDING TO MAORI HISTORY, SOMETIME DURING THE tenth century A.D., a Polynesian navigator named Kupe sailed from an island in the vicinity of Tahiti in search of a land to the south, "uninhabited and covered with mists." Kupe apparently found his way through the mists and back again to his native island, called Hawaiaki. Approximately four centuries later, emboldened by the legend of Kupe and driven by a need to migrate due to intertribal warfare, ten canoes filled with intrepid Hawaiakians set out for Kupe's southern site. Just as Christopher Columbus's ships, the *Pinta, Niña* and *Santa Maria,* are part of the legend of the "discovery" of America, the names of the ten canoes are recorded in Maori history. The names of the crews are also remembered, and—like the descendants of those who came to America on the

Mayflower—the Maoris trace their lineage back to those who arrived during this particular migration. Kupe named this new world Aotearoa, "the land of the long white cloud." This was the last major land mass to be reached and inhabited by man.

It was three hundred years before the "Vikings of the sunrise," who came to be known as the Maoris, were visited by the Dutch explorer Abel Janszoon Tasman. Tasman sailed from what is now Jakarta, Indonesia, where the Dutch East India Company had established itself as a trading mecca, around Australia, to Kupe's port. Commanding two ships, the *Heemskerck* and *Zeehaen,* in an effort to find a more expeditious route to the Spanish trading grounds at Chile, following the landmark forays of Balboa, Magellan, Mendana, Quiros and Drake, Tasman encountered this unexpected land mass. A Maori canoe intercepted a boat traveling between Tasman's two ships that were anchored in what came to be called Murderers Bay, in commemoration of this incident, and a battle ensued, resulting in a number of Tasman's crew being captured, brought ashore and cooked and eaten. Tasman took flight to Tonga, but he charted the Maori area, which led to the ultimate change on Dutch maps from "Staten Landt," their name for South America, to "Nieuw Zeelandt," or "Nieuw Zeeland," after the Dutch island province of Zeeland.

The stage was set for Captain James Cook, the British seafarer who rounded Cape Horn and sailed into the Pacific Ocean just after the New Year in 1769. Ten months later the ship's boy of Cook's boat *The Endeavour*, Nicholas Young, spotted the coast of North Island, New Zealand, at a point known ever since as Young Nick's Head. It was Cook who named the Bay of Islands.

Cook's initial landing resulted in a violent episode similar to that experienced by Tasman more than a century before; but eventually Cook's party accomplished an exchange of goods with the Maoris, toured a Maori village and, of course, claimed the land for England.

Cook's circumnavigation of both the North and South islands provided a workable chart of the coastline, and his six months' stay allowed the two botanists he'd brought along on the expedition ample opportunity to study the indigenous plant life. Cook returned to New Zealand several times during three subsequent expeditions, with no untoward incidents, spending more than two months there at a time.

Polynesian peoples emigrated not only to New Zealand, certainly, but to Madagascar, Indonesia, Malaysia, the Philippines, Japan and elsewhere. Auckland calls itself "the largest Polynesian city in the world." Those from Hawaiaki, in all likelihood, also traveled to and settled in Hawaii, the latter name being a variation of the former. It was in Hawaii that Cook was stabbed to death by the natives, those cousins of the Maoris, less than a decade after his initial glimpse of the Pacific Ocean.

After Cook came more British, the French (among them de Surville, from whose name the word *surveillance* is derived; and du Fresne, whose murder by the Maoris caused a retaliation resulting in the slaughter of 250 of them at the hands of French sailors), the Italians and the Spanish. The Maori word for European is *pakeh*—tantamount to *gaijin* in Japanese, *gringo* in Spanish, *low fon* in Chinese. The White Ghosts had come to stay, but most of the contact between Maoris and Europeans, as well as with the Americans, took place due to the whaling trade. The principal meeting place was at Kororareka—Maori for "sweet little blue penguin"—in the Bay of Islands. The quiet town of Russell.

3.

RUSSELL, DUBBED BY MISSIONARIES OF THE EARLY nineteenth century the "hell-hole of the Pacific," was a sailor's paradise. Populated by fugitives of all kinds, prostitutes, rum and musket runners, the Maoris of the Bay of Islands were quickly exposed to the various evils of the white world. The Maoris, however, did their bit to set race relations back when in 1809 a group of them, in response to the flogging of a Maori deckhand, burned the British ship *Boyd,* then murdered and devoured her crew. The white whalers of the Bay of Islands took revenge on the Maoris shortly thereafter by slaughtering several dozen of them, including a tribal leader considered to have been responsible for the *Boyd* incident.

In 1830, the "War of the Girls" erupted when two Maori maidens from separate tribes contested for the affections of a *pakeha* whaling-boat skipper. The two tribes fought each other until the head chief of all the Maoris, Titore, created a new border separating the tribal territories.

Ten years later, however, the British Crown dispatched Captain William Hobson to the Bay of Islands where, on the sixth of February 1840, he signed a treaty with—and *for*—forty-five Maori chiefs at Waitangi. It is this date that is recognized as the birth of modern New Zealand. Auckland was soon thereafter named the new capital—a distinction that has since passed to Wellington, on the South Island—supplanting Russell.

It was not long before all hell broke loose. Hone Heke, the principal chief to allow Hobson to sign for him the famous treaty at Waitangi, chopped down the flagstaff that flew the Union Jack at Russell. The British government's attempt to set itself up as go-between in all Maori-*pakeha* deals proved a disaster, and the Maoris collectively decided to opt out of the agreement.

What ensued was a full-scale war that was waged concurrent with the War Between the States in America. The results of both conflicts were virtually the same: The Maoris, like the Confederacy, were ultimately defeated by superior manpower and armaments. One of the principal points of dispute was that the Maoris considered the sale of their land to the Europeans to have involved only a transfer of the *shadow* of the land, not the actual property, a concept the *pakehas* did not readily grasp.

4.

THE LAND OF THE LONG WHITE CLOUD PASSED FOR THE time being into the hands of its new conquerors; but the Creation, say the Maoris, still and forever will belong to them. Billy Boy Reynolds, for one, was fond of repeating the story of how Rangi, the sky father, and Papa, the earth mother, brought forth from Te Po, the long dark night, Tane, their eldest son, god of the forests. Tane bedecked Rangi with the sun, moon and stars, Billy Boy would say; Papa he imbued with all plant and animal life. Rangi, according to Billy Boy's version of the events, was saddened by having been separated from Papa, so he began to cry. His tears filled her crevices with streams, rivers, lakes and oceans. How the fish got into the waters was a mystery, said Billy Boy, but he had a theory: Tane threw them in after he'd seen the result of Rangi's outpouring of grief. Billy Boy, who'd had plenty of grief in his own life, used to say that sadness, or the effort to avoid sadness, is the supreme motivator of mankind.

The night before Billy Boy was found dead on the porch, he had gotten stinking drunk, first at a dinner dance, and then continued his run at the Swordfish

Club bar. Not only did he repeat at the club several times over the Maori creation myth, but, according to Moss Hawks, a fellow charter boat captain and long-time mate of his who was there, Billy Boy drunkenly declaimed that the seas around New Zealand, and particularly the Bay of Islands, were populated by *marakihau,* ancestral spirits of the Maoris who have adopted the form of mermen. These creatures, said Billy Boy, are reptiles with curled tails, horned heads and cylindrical tongues. The *marakihau* were capable of devouring whole ships and their crews. "One of these days soon," Billy Boy announced to the others at the Swordfish Club bar, staggering from the effects of a long evening of drinking, "they'll grab and eat the lot of you *pakehas.* Then we'll take it all back, the land and the sea."

Moss Hawks and Hunt Terry, who'd also been present, both told Liam Jones, the Russell policeman, that they'd never heard Billy Boy talk like that before. Liam Jones said that since there was no weapon found at the scene, and Billy Boy's hands yielded no evidence of powder burns, his death was obviously not a suicide. "Maybe somebody in the bar got ticked off at the way Billy Boy was blathering about all that Maori shit," said

Hunt. "I could see somebody belting him over it," said Moss, "but not shooting him." "Well, somebody shot him," Liam Jones said. "Didn't they?"

5.

THE NEWS AT THE TIME OF BILLY BOY'S MURDER WAS FULL of the Kanak rebel activities in New Caledonia. The New Zealand *Herald* reported the day before that Captain Philippe Legorjus, the commander of France's elite antiterrorist forces, had been kidnapped by the separatists and was being held on the remote island of Ouvea. New Caledonia is part of the French Overseas Territories, and reinforcements in the form of 250 naval infantrymen and ninety extra gendarmes were being dispatched to Noumea, the capital. Bernard Pons, the French minister sent to Ouvea to consult with the government leaders, said that the leader of the rebels was "a sort of religious fanatic" who had been one of the first members of the Kanak Socialist National Liberation Front to be sent to Libya for military training. The separatists, according to the *Herald,* had vowed to maintain a state of "permanent insecurity" in the French South

Pacific Territory if their demands for independence were not met. The capture of Captain Legorjus and his aides brought to twenty-three the number of French hostages held by the Kanaks.

On the front page of the newspaper was a photograph of an armed, hooded Kanak kneeling behind a fence post on watch near Canala, sixty kilometers north of Noumea. The spokesman for the Kanak was described in the *Herald* as also wearing a hood and holding a rifle. The pockets of his field jacket were filled with cartridges. There were problems of a similar nature occurring throughout Melanesia, said the paper. New Guinea and Fiji were also "experiencing some unrest," and in Auckland there had recently been a highly publicized incident involving a Maori woman's "kill a white a day" speech given at a local university.

Moss Hawks read the *Herald* article aloud to his wife, Roxanne, the afternoon following the discovery of Billy Boy's body. "Do you think it's this kind of stuff got Billy Boy going?" Moss asked her.

6.

AT THE SATURDAY NIGHT DINNER DANCE BENEFIT FOR THE Russell School Sports Club, Billy Boy Reynolds discovered his wife, Jane, kissing Curly Whitehall outside against the back wall of the Wharf Hotel. Jane Reynolds told the inspectors from Whangarei, whom Liam Jones had brought in to investigate the case, that Curly and Billy Boy had a brief fistfight that ended in Billy Boy's being knocked down a couple of times.

"Billy Boy was already drunk," Jane said. "He and Curly never did get on well. Curly and I were only just having an innocent nuzzle, a bit of fun during the party, that's all. Billy Boy got too carried away and Curly had to punch him; though Curly held off really doing Billy Boy any serious damage because of his condition. If you ask me, Curly was quite within his rights, even though I am—or was—Billy Boy's wife."

7.

"BILLY BOY TOLD ME ONCE THAT THE MAORIS USED TO fish from canoes using a stingray attached to a long pole as a teaser to attract mako sharks," Moss Hawks told the inspectors. "He said they'd splash the ray up and down and when they got a shark suckered in alongside they'd lasso its tail and then sit back and let it tow them through the water. The Maoris would all kneel together in the center of the canoe so the shark could spin freely, and when the thing got tired out they'd hurl their spears into it.

"Billy Boy also told me he learned about using gin bottles as teasers from Hunko Hollins, a guide out of Whitianga. I think it was Hunko who taught Billy Boy the art of emptying the gin bottle first. Billy Boy never had a shortage of them.

"He knew all sorts of things. Billy Boy was never shy about sharing his knowledge with anyone who seemed genuinely interested in what he had to say. He told me that marlin bite best two days before a storm; and that a pregnant shark will dump its babies when it's hooked. I remembered this second bit of information one day when I was in a shark contest: I shoved a rolled-up newspaper into a shark's hole because I wanted to preserve its weight. Billy Boy showed me how to invent a lure out of a length of hose; he taught me that there's no point in trolling in a layer of cold water on top if you can put a bait into warm water down below.

"Billy Boy was a hunter," said Moss. "He knew how to catch fish. But he was an honest hunter, I think, and a considerate one, if there is such a thing. I know, for example, that Billy Boy always used galvanized hooks rather than those made of stainless steel. Soft steel hooks have a better point, even if you have to sharpen them every time; but Billy Boy used them because if a fish gets away the galvanized hook will deteriorate rapidly, whereas the stainless steel one will be stuck in the fish forever. He was a sportsman.

"Billy Boy never hard-baited, either. He never made the tie through the eye of the hook around the tail of the baitfish unbreakable if he could help it. He said if you made it absolutely unbreakable then the bait would lodge sideways in the fish's throat and choke it to death. In Billy Boy's mind this wasn't the correct way to go about things. He also hated backing-down on fish with the boat, so that all the angler has to do is reel in slack line. 'That's not angling,' Billy Boy would say, 'that's murder.'"

8.

Curly Whitehall, when questioned by the police, was less than enthusiastic about the charms of Billy Boy Reynolds. "He was a rotten drunk and wife-beater," Curly said. "Jane told me that he'd get pissed almost every night and knock her about.

"He used to be considered a pretty good fisherman," Curly told the cops, "one of the best hereabouts, actually. I know when he was a kid Billy Boy became famous in Russell for a fight he had with a mako shark that weighed over five hundred pounds. My father told me about it, so it must be true. Billy Boy, who was about fifteen years old, harpooned this mako and the critter went wild. Another angler on board decided to shoot it, so he picked up a rifle and fired a .303 bullet. The fool shot the trace right off the hook, and Billy Boy had to land that mako with the harpoon line, which he somehow managed to do. That became a kind of legendary incident around here.

"But I know Billy Boy lost a lot of his charter customers over the last few years due to his drinking. He used to fish with a doctor from Los Angeles for a month every year, Dr. Anderson. Billy Boy had him eight or nine years straight, marlin fishing, and they used to average at least half a dozen marlin a week. Dr. Anderson told me they once caught eighteen in six days. It was Dr. Anderson who landed a blue marlin that weighed more than 750 pounds, close to the record for New Zealand. The doctor quit fishing with Billy Boy a couple of years back, though; one by one all his regular customers went off him. I picked up two or three and he probably hated my guts for that, but it was his own fault.

"As far as my playing around with Jane is concerned, it never went any further than a little good-natured pashing. You know, nothing serious. I sure as hell didn't shoot the bastard, though I can't say I'm sorry it happened. That's about it from my point of view."

9.

WHILE THE WHANGAREI COPPERS CONDUCTED THEIR investigation, Moss Hawks decided to see what he could find out on his own. "Maybe I can pick up some information that will help," Moss said to Roxanne. "After all, I know just about everyone in Russell."

"Be careful," Roxanne told him. "You never know

what you don't want to know until you know it, and then it's too late."

What Roxanne didn't know was that Moss and Jane Reynolds had been lovers on an intermittent basis for the last couple of years. It was Jane whom Moss went to see first.

"I was wondering when I'd get to see your silly face again," Jane said when she let Moss into the house.

"Silly, is it?" said Moss.

"So what is it, darling?" Jane asked. "Have you come to tell me now that Billy Boy's dead you're going to divorce Roxanne and marry me?"

"That wouldn't look too good, would it now?" said Moss. "I mean with Billy Boy only barely beginning to get cold."

Jane laughed. "As if you'd do such a thing, anyway," she said.

"Now, now, Janie love. You know we couldn't get along for more than four or five days without one of us ending up like Billy Boy."

"Never know until you try," said Jane. "Then why have you come?" she asked. "I haven't seen you for weeks."

"Ten days," said Moss.

"All right, ten days. Why?"

"I heard that Billy Boy was shot with a .38," Moss said. "Hunt Terry heard it from Liam Jones."

"Yes, so?"

"Do you still have that old army pistol I gave you? The Webley."

"That gun you told me could shoot only around corners?"

Moss wasn't laughing. "I gave it to you to scare off Billy Boy when he got too drunk and began to threaten you. It was a .38."

"Was it?" said Jane. "I'd forgotten, if I ever knew. I don't know where it's gotten to, if you want to know the truth. I haven't seen it in ages. And besides, you never gave me any bullets for it."

"You never misplaced anything in your life, Jane. Where's the gun?"

"I told you, I don't know."

"Did you give it to Curly?"

"You'd better leave," Jane said. "You'd better go before I say I never want to see you again."

"I'm going to have to talk to Curly, Jane, unless you tell me."

"Go on, then. Ask Curly. I told you I don't know anything about the gun. I don't know where it is. If I find it, I'll put it in a box and send it to you because I think I *don't* want to see you again. At least for a while. Really, Moss, I'm the grieving widow, for God's sake. Leave me alone."

10.

MOSS LOOKED AT HIS MAORI FISH CALENDAR AND READ the forecast for the next day: "Ouenukie—Good from dawn to midday. Good for eels at night." He decided to accept a half-day charter and to go see Curly in the late afternoon.

On his way home Moss spotted Johnnie Hudspeth leaning on the gate in front of his house on the waterfront. Moss went over to say hello. It was Johnnie Hudspeth who'd helped Moss get started as a fishing guide fourteen years before. Johnnie was now in his late seventies or early eighties, and he didn't fish anymore.

Johnnie had fished for five months in Tahiti with Zane Grey during the 1920s. He became famous for having been the only skipper to have had a triple strike on marlin with one angler aboard and boated all of them. In one season Johnnie had caught ninety-five marlin, one of them a 925-pound black; and he was in his own category for having captured a half dozen of the rare broadbill swordfish during his lifetime. Johnnie had held his marine ticket for sixty years, a local record.

Born at Whangaroa in a building that was known as the Kiwi's Nest, one of the first hotels in New Zealand, Johnnie had been raised on a farm in Rawhiti. Drawn to the sea, he escaped the land at his first opportunity after working for a time in the Portland Cement Works near Whangarei and saving enough money to buy his first fishing boat. Moss often stopped by to talk with Johnnie and listen to his stories about the old days.

"We used to go out hunting for sharks," Johnnie told Moss, "because they were prized for their teeth. The marlin were about like flies but we didn't know what they were and we used to try to harpoon them!

"It was Zane Grey that landed the first broadbill in the Bay, a four-hundred-pounder, I believe, in about 1926. After that a whole bunch were caught. It was Grey who showed the way, I guess. He was a hell of a fish-erman. He brought over all kinds of gear from America that nobody'd seen before: wide Coxe reels, stubby hickory rods with guides narrowly spaced, Ashaway lines, Pflueger hooks and nicely designed harnesses. Grey insisted on trolling rather than drifting; *creating* a situation to attract the fish, using teasers to give the impression to anything down below that there's a school of fish up above. Grey liked to *see* his fish, to hook him in the jaw and stop him as short as possible, then sit back and enjoy the show. Hooking the fish in the mouth, Grey showed us, is what's accomplished by trolling, as opposed to the gut-hooking that occurs by drifting. Hooking them in the mouth makes the fish jump.

"I remember when Grey hooked a broadbill about nine miles north of Ninepin Rock. This fish played deep for more than half an hour and then surfaced, flinging its tail in the air before diving straight down like a cannonball. There was no way Grey could raise the fish, and eventually we had to handline it. It came up tail first, tangled in the trace, and with the spear muddied to behind the eyes with its lower jaw torn loose. The fish had driven hard into the mud and stuck there until it died. The spear on this broadbill was more than five feet long! I believe it weighed almost six hundred pounds.

"The last broadbill I handled myself," said Johnnie, "was the toughest. We circled the fish for an hour and tried every trick we knew to make it take one of the trolls. Finally I pulled in one of the lines and stuck a fresh *kahawai* on it, moved in close and *threw* the bait at him! I reckon I insulted him by doing this and he went at it, swallowing it down. He came up pretty easy after that, all four hundred pounds of him."

Moss was pleased to find Johnnie so talkative. Johnnie's daughter, Marella, had told Moss a week or so before that her father had been having some bad spells lately due to his emphysema. There weren't too many of the Bay of Islands pioneer fishermen left. Francis Arlidge, another old-timer who had fished with Zane Grey, had recently passed away. Arlidge, too, had helped Moss establish himself as a guide. Moss never passed up an opportunity to visit with Johnnie now, since he never knew which one would be the last.

11.

MOSS STOPPED IN AT THE SWORDFISH CLUB FOR A QUICK beer and was surprised to see Honey Cooney, another old-timer, standing at the bar with a couple of regulars.

Honey greeted Moss effusively and pumped Moss's hand with the grip of a much younger man.

"Thought I'd come and take a look around the scene of the crime," said Honey. "I was just explaining to these boys how Johnnie Hudspeth and I used to make our fishing poles when we were mates in Whangaroa. We'd get our sticks out of the bush, *tanehaka* wood, or *manuka;* but *manuka* wasn't as strong as the *tanehaka* saplings, which grow up straight as a dart, close-grained and sturdy. We'd submerge them in a creek to drain the sap from them, which took a couple of months. We'd soak them in oil after that, douse it through proper for a few weeks. I'd take a length of drainpipe, plug up one end, stand it upright and fill it with linseed oil. When it was done you had a rod that would last a lifetime. It was a big improvement over the light split-cane poles the English fishermen used."

Honey paused to finish off his pint of beer, ordered another and continued his narrative.

"The English reels, too, were all wrong for fishing anything but trout or salmon, not for deep-sea fishing. The old reels were huge in diameter but skinny and mounted under the rod. Zane Grey, of course, changed the philosophy over here. Those old reels had no clutch, no brake, only two little knobs on the side, one of which you grabbed to wind. If you didn't grab quickly enough all your knuckles were torn off. I used one of these for a while and the first joint on my little finger was never the same again. Later on, a leather brake was invented that operated on a gearing system similar in principle to that of the Model T Ford. Must have made anglers with paralyzed hands happier! And the lines, of course, were made of linen, which had to be dried out after every outing. We used 'gang hooks' then, triple hooks on each line. Grey, again, apparently thought this was unfair to the fish; and after he made his presence felt, anglers began using a single hook.

"For bait we used whatever anyone thought best. Maybe cut bait, maybe whole. I'll never forget one day we'd fished off Bora-Bora in a fancy boat using highly sophisticated gear and trying a wide variety of highly recommended lures and not raised a fin. Heading in we passed a guy in a dinghy propelled by a dinky outboard. He was sitting back smoking a cigarette while he putt-putted along, enjoying the sunset and easy sea. Balanced across the thwarts of his little craft was one of the largest blue marlin I've ever seen. That evening I located this fellow on shore and congratulated him on his catch. What I wanted to know, I told him, was how he'd done it. He didn't think much of my question or his method, but he was gracious enough to indulge me.

"He used a very long, heavy handline, he said; heavy not so much for strength but because it was easier on his hands. On the end was a sinker, a wire leader and a large single hook. He'd let out about a couple of hundred yards of line and wait. Once a fish was hooked, the fellow explained, you just let him tow you around the ocean with the line on a fairlead on the bow. If you got a slack line you pulled it in. There was no hurry. By the time the fish came up he was tired out and you could pull him over the stern if he wasn't too heavy; otherwise you towed him, which was a bother because it wasted fuel. The kicker here came when I asked him what he used for bait. 'A chunk of rotten meat,' the guy said. 'It was going to be tossed away,' he told me, and he thought there was no sense in wasting it. So much for all our modern techniques!"

Honey wanted to know all about the murder of Billy Boy Reynolds, but there wasn't much Moss could tell him, or wanted to. The crime was the biggest news at the Swordfish Club since Zane Grey arrived sixty-nine years before, and then all he killed were fish.

12.

MOSS KNEW CURLY WOULD NOT BE HAPPY TO SEE HIM. They'd never been the best of mates, though they got along well enough. Each of them knew of the other's interest in Jane Reynolds, but they'd never discussed her. She was—or had been—Billy Boy's wife, so what was there to talk about?

Curly lived on a small plot of land up the Waikeri Inlet, a barely navigable backwater where visitors were generally unwelcome. The few people who lived there guarded their privacy actively; most had stills where they brewed their own beer or whisky, and several were known to have cultivated sizeable marijuana crops. Curly's place resembled an alligator hunter's shack in a Louisiana bayou. A large sign posted at the front of the property warned: KEEP GOING.

Curly had made his living for the past twenty-five years as his father had for thirty years before him, by netting flounder that he sold for baitfish at the Russell wharf. Every morning from six to about ten-thirty or eleven, Curly could be found reeling in his fine mesh nets in the bay, separating out the *kahawai* and snapper from the flounder. His long, sinewy forearms were extremely powerful from the years of sustained net-pulling. He had a well-earned reputation as a hard drinker and rough customer. Curly kept pretty much to himself, however, on his homestead, where he lived with a milk cow, some chickens, a few goats, a pig and several nasty dogs. He'd built a smokehouse where he cooked the *kahawai* that comprised the staple of his diet other than the poultry and dairy products procured from his animals. Curly had been busted for growing weed several years before, and he spent six months in jail for it. Moss knew that Curly had been married for a while and had some kids, but he'd heard that the wife and children had gone off following Curly's arrest to live in Auckland.

Moss came in quietly on his launch, the *Yellowtail Two,* to Curly's shore, cutting his engine and drifting close to the gravel beach, where he was immediately set upon by a pack of lean, snarling, barking dogs. He'd been thinking on the way over about a different kind of murder that still went senselessly on, the killing of game fish, especially billfish, of which there were too few left. Due to the prevalence of longline commercial fishing operations, the time when sports fishermen could expect to catch at least one or more good-sized marlin in the Bay of Islands on any particular day was fast becoming a distant memory.

This last week the Duke of Marlborough International Billfish Tournament at Russell had seemed to Moss like a sick joke, a kind of slapstick tragedy. The few marlin reeled in by pot-bellied, rich businessmen had been hung up and weighed on the dock to no good purpose. These fish should have been tagged and released, Moss believed, in order not only to preserve these great specimens, but to study the migration habits of pelagic species. Legislation was being enforced to limit the long-liners but it seemed, unfortunately, like closing the barn door after the horses had escaped. There were just too few billfish left to endure this silliness of the angler posing on the dock with a beer in one hand and the other clutching the great dead fish's dorsal fin. What good was that trophy now? Moss was disgusted by the whole thing; among charter boat captains he found himself in the distinct minority concerning tagging versus landing billfish, and he had to be careful what he said around the Swordfish Club, but he couldn't help half the time wishing it were the angler hanging on the scales instead of the fish.

Moss waited in the *Yellowtail Two* just offshore far enough that the dogs couldn't reach him. Curly would be out soon to call them off. Moss had been here once before, and that was to take a look at an outboard motor Curly was selling a year or so ago. From what Moss could make out in the moonlight, the shorefront area looked about the same as it had before: an ancient, rusted-out, blackened tugboat set up on blocks; piles of planks and wire; old tires; automobile parts; rusted bedsprings; broken appliances; stove-in dinghies; ripped-up sofas and busted chairs, and so on. It was your basic junkyard. The air reeked of smoked fish. Moss could see a thin trail of smoke coming from the shack just on shore that Curly used for that purpose. Curly always smelled of smoked fish; it was an unmistakable odor and one that was virtually impossible to mask.

Living in a small town like Russell, Moss thought, suited him, at least the convenience of everything. The general store, the hardware and fish supply shops and the Swordfish Club were no more than a three-minute walk from his house, as was the boat ramp. He recalled a story Johnnie Hudspeth had told him about the days in Whangaroa when that town was so small there were only two cars in it, and they had a collision! Sometimes life seems like that, thought Moss. If there's any chance of the sky falling on you, it will. Best to keep your head covered just in case.

Moss saw Curly's tall, lanky shape approaching from the house. He was holding a rifle and when he was about ten yards from the shore Curly lifted it and leveled the barrel at Moss. The dogs were still snarling and growling and Curly made no attempt to quiet them.

"What do you want?" Curly shouted over the canine chorus.

"To talk," said Moss.

"If it's about Billy Boy, I've told everything I know to the cops. I've nothing to say to you, anyhow."

Curly kicked at the dogs to stop them from howling.

"It would be best if you'd just start up your motor," Curly told Moss. "You'd better take off."

"I've been to see Jane," Moss said. "Do you have the gun I gave her?"

Curly kept the rifle pointed at Moss. "That's enough, Moss," Curly said. "Get started now before I sink your boat and you've got to swim home."

Moss cranked his engine and slowly came about. He'd have his day with Curly Stillwell, Moss thought. There was no mistake about that.

13.

THE RAIN WOKE MOSS JUST BEFORE DAWN. IT HAD BEEN almost a month since the last measurable downpour and Moss stood watching the rain through his kitchen window. He'd been upset when he returned home the night before from his encounter with Curly, and he stayed up late reading his father's well-thumbed copy of C. Alma Baker's *Rough Guide to New Zealand Big Game Fishing.*

Self-published in 1937, Baker's book had been the only one other than the Bible that Moss could remember his father reading. Baker, who'd spent most of his life as a rubber planter in Malaya, was a character straight out of a Somerset Maugham novel. Always impeccably dressed and exhibiting the finest manners, Baker was an avid fisherman who persuaded Zane Grey to come to the Bay of Islands. Baker and Grey had stayed together in Waipiro Bay before Grey established his own camp at Otehei Bay. Baker designed a hook which was manufactured and sold by Hardy Brothers of London, and in 1916 he fashioned a reel which he claimed was the only two-geared, free spot design then available. Baker became a member of the Swordfish Club in the early 1920s, and later served as vice president. The coastal waters of New Zealand became his favorite part of the world. Moss felt that much of the ground covered by Baker more than fifty years ago was still of value for anglers today. The section he'd read the night before was "When a Big Fellow Is Hooked."

"When a fish is hooked," Baker wrote, "it must be allowed to finish its first mad rush and turn the bait before the angler attempts to reel in the slack line preparatory to driving home the hook. One—two—three; the line comes taught as a fiddle string; often the fish leaps high into the air. The Captain swings the wheel to follow him; the spare man takes the removable back out of the swivel chair, and stands to turn it in the direction of the fight, as with a heavy hard fighting fish it is very difficult for the fisherman to turn it himself. Now all is ready for the battle, which may last for anything up to six hours. A striped marlin from 200 to 300 pounds often takes from an hour to two hours to bring to gaff, and big black marlin, broadbill or the larger sharks, will, of course, take considerably longer.

"Line is best recovered in the fight," Baker suggested, "by short, quick 'pumps,' which keeps the fish's head towards the boat. Sometimes only a quarter turn of the reel handle, sometimes more, can be taken on the quick drop of the rod from a low pump. Very often the fish will allow nothing to be taken. The red binding at the top of the double line is anxiously looked for in a long fight; this is taken over the reel many times, only to be turned out again by the fighting fish; but even when the fish is fairly beaten, and the trace is grasped to gaff it, many things may happen to prevent it being brought aboard, and the fish is by no means yours until the tail chain is securely snugged over the tail, and the fish made fast to the bollards on the 'counter.' Then, and only then, can the fisherman call the fish his and fly the fishing flag of victory from the masthead."

Moss's father, Boyd Hawks, had known Alma Baker through their association in the Swordfish Club. Boyd told Moss that Baker had fished right to the end of his life. In his last outing, Boyd said, Baker hooked an average-weight striped marlin. When the fish went deep and died, however, Baker refused to accept any help to lift it and the sharks got to it; only the head, vertebrae and tail came to the boat. Another old man and the sea story, Moss thought, but a true one.

14.

THERE WAS A GUY MOSS HAD SEEN PERIODICALLY OVER the last few months hanging around the waterfront, sitting on the wharf or walking through town, whom he knew nothing about other than that the man's name was Jeff and he was an American. Jeff looked to be in his mid-forties; he had a weather-beaten face, as if he spent most of his time out of doors. He had long, greasy hair, a short beard and mustache, and always wore a blue Greek fisherman's cap and carried a small, well-worn canvas sack over one shoulder.

Moss mentioned Jeff to his friend Woolly Larrabee, who, with his wife Faith, owned and operated the Russell Arms Hotel. Woolly and Faith were refugees from Liverpool, part of the third of that economically devastated city's population who'd fled the north of England in search of a future. Woolly told Moss that he had spoken with Jeff on a couple of occasions and learned that he was your basic South Seas drifter. Originally from Los Angeles, Jeff had left the United States mainland during the Vietnam war and never gone back. He traveled throughout the South Pacific mostly by boat, working on private yachts and occasionally on freighters. Jeff would do odd jobs wherever he landed: in Honolulu, he worked for a car-rental outfit; in Papeete, he washed dishes; in Auckland, he managed a roller-skating rink; in Melbourne, he worked as a car mechanic. He'd come to Russell on a sailboat, crewing for a clothing-store magnate from Wellington. Jeff liked the place and decided to stay for as long as he could afford to. Woolly told Moss that he didn't know where Jeff lived, if he lived anywhere.

"I think he probably just camps out down the beach

somewhere," Woolly said. "Why are you so interested in him?"

"I saw him talking to Billy Boy once," Moss said. "Arguing, really. They were down in front of the Swordy and I was up on the porch with Monty. It was about a week before Billy Boy was murdered."

"What were they going on about?"

"I couldn't tell. I meant to ask Billy Boy about it later but never got round to it."

"Maybe Monty knows something," Woolly offered. "Ask him."

Moss mentioned Jeff and the argument with Billy Boy to Monty the next time he saw him. Monty Cricklewood and his wife Gretchen were originally from London; they made a decent living in Russell as taxidermists, transforming gamefish into mounted trophies for anglers. Monty fashioned the models and Gretchen painted them. Neither of them had ever seen a game fish prior to settling down in Russell. They'd come on a visit, liked the place, decided to stay on if they could and bought the taxidermy business. Gretchen's initial efforts were based on the colors of fish as they were represented in picture books, a fact she enjoyed joking about now that she and Monty were old hands at the game. Gretchen was always pregnant; she and Monty had been married for nine years and they had five children. Monty, naturally enough, was always worried about money.

"Do you remember Billy Boy and this fellow Jeff having at it in front of the club?" Moss asked.

"Not really," Monty said. "I did see Jeff—that's his name?" Moss nodded. "On Billy Boy's boat, it was. They were headed out toward Waikeri. I guess they were going to Billy Boy's place."

"Was that before or after we saw them arguing?" Moss asked.

"It must have been before that," said Monty. "Had to have been, because I was delivering that blue marlin head to Paihia when I saw them going out."

"Thanks, Monty. How's Gretchen?"

"She thinks she's pregnant again. I'm thinking of going back to the oil company I used to work for in Aussie. I can certainly make more money as a radiographer than I can mounting fish. The problem is they'd ship me out to Saudi again for four months, and I couldn't take that. Locked up in an Aramco compound with a bunch of

Texans, having to listen to all that horrible piped-in country-and-western music. And the Saudis are worse. If you're involved in a traffic accident there, even if it isn't your fault you go to jail because it wouldn't have happened if you hadn't been there. Know what I mean? Irrefutable logic of the bloody place. Allah willed it, you see. Ah, Moss, don't get me going."

Monty was a small, nervous man with a thin, greying beard. He had a gentle face sparked by bright blue eyes. His sense of humor saved him.

"Sorry, Moss," he said, lighting a cigarette. "I'll work it out somehow, as usual."

"No problem, mate," Moss laughed. "Let me know if you need a loan."

Monty shook his head. "Thanks. I'll handle it. You reckon this Jeff had something to do with what happened to Billy Boy, do you?"

"I don't know," said Moss. "But I figure we ought to find out."

15.

WOOLLY LARRABEE WAS AN ARTIST; SOMETHING OF A frustrated one at present, however, due to his having to spend most of his time running the hotel rather than drawing and painting. He'd attended art college in Liverpool—the same one John Lennon went to, he told everyone proudly, five years after the future Beatle—and had a bona fide, devilishly clever Liverpudlian sense of humor. Woolly's real name was Arthur; he'd been called Woolly ever since he'd grown his bushy red-brown beard at the age of twenty. He was a seemingly tireless individual, constantly drumming up business for the hotel, engaging every other person on the street in animated conversation, chain-smoking, dashing in and out of the Swordfish Club for beers and shots of Irish whisky and games of eight-ball, cooking up big Indian dinners for Faith and himself and their friends, painting pictures, swatting at the old Gibson country-and-western acoustic guitar he'd never properly learned to play, doing a little carpentry work on the side or helping Monty Cricklewood with the taxidermy when one of Gretchen's pregnancies prevented her from working. In addition to all this, Woolly was an avid and quite competent fisherman, often accompanying Moss Hawks on forays in the bay.

Faith Larrabee tended to the two children and made certain the bills were paid. Woolly's gregarious behavior was good for business and Faith rather liked his artwork; though it frightened her a little whenever he got fed up with the hotel and threatened to sell it and do nothing but paint. She and Gretchen Cricklewood and Roxanne Hawks were very close friends. They liked living in Russell, the civilized atmosphere, and all of the wives were shocked by the murder of Billy Boy Reynolds, even though Billy Boy and Jane had not been part of their inner circle. Faith spent most of her free time reading literary novels, which distinguished her from the other wives, none of whom read anything more taxing than the Sunday newspaper or women's housekeeping and fashion magazines. At the moment, Faith was halfway through *Mrs Palfrey at the Claremont* by Elizabeth Taylor (the English novelist, not the American actress). Taylor, she decided, was a good writer, a truth teller, but not the prose stylist nor as authentic in her concerns as her contemporary Jean Rhys. Faith was not unflattered that she and Woolly were considered the "arty" couple in the crowd.

When Jane Reynolds called Faith and asked to meet her at the Verandah for lunch the next day, something she'd never done before, Faith was more than a little surprised. When she mentioned it to Woolly, he joked that since Billy Boy was gone Jane now had more time on her hands and probably just wanted Faith to recommend a good book.

16.

Moss had a half-day charter, a family from Auckland whom he took snapper and kahawai fishing off the Cavalli Islands. After returning them to the wharf at Russell, Moss went back across the bay to the marine supply store at Whangarei to pick up a new Furuno fish finder he'd ordered. In the old days he would have stopped in at the pub in Whangarei, but in the last couple of years it had been taken over by a Maori gang called the Down-and-Out Boys, familiarly referred to as DO-Boys. The DO-Boys wore colors similar to the Hell's Angels and they rode motorcycles like their American counterparts, after whom they'd modeled their organization. The difference between them was that the DO-Boys were exclusively composed of Maoris who considered themselves blacks, the underclass of New Zealand. This gang specialized in drug dealing and protection rackets, and was blatantly unfriendly toward *pakehas,* whom they considered colonial oppressors. In the countrywide race war soon to come, the DO-Boys believed, the Maoris would reclaim the lands and fishing grounds that were rightfully theirs, which the whites had stolen from their ancestors.

Moss saw the motorbikes lined up outside the pub and asked Derek Smyth, the marine supply store owner, if there had been much trouble lately in Whangarei.

"Not really, Moss," Derek said. "Actually, I reckon the DO-Boys are plotting something sizeable. It's been too quiet and of course the cops are afraid to rock the boat. By the way, I heard about Billy Boy Reynolds being found murdered at the Swordy."

"Three days ago," Moss said. "Someone shot him in the head."

"Well, I saw him here, you know. Must have been no more than a week ago. He was coming out of the pub with that DO-Boy they call Mister Mongrel, one of their leaders."

"I didn't know Billy Boy had dealings with them," said Moss.

Derek nodded. "They were pretty familiar-seeming, Billy Boy and this Mongrel. I noticed when Billy Boy left they did that funny fist-knocking handshake the Maori gangs all do. And they were in high spirits about something, both of them laughing."

"Thanks for telling me about this, Derek."

"Glad to be of help, mate. Hope they find out who killed Billy Boy."

"It's getting more complicated all the time," said Moss. "At least so far as I'm concerned."

17.

JANE REYNOLDS WAS ALREADY SEATED AT A TABLE IN THE Verandah restaurant when Faith Larrabee arrived. The two women greeted each other cordially, and, since the waiter appeared almost immediately following Faith, they ordered lunch.

"I'd like to tell you what I've learned about wives," Jane said.

Faith was amused by this opener. It was worthy of

Doris Lessing, she thought, or Margaret Atwood, if not Jean Rhys. Faith smiled and said, "I'd like to hear it."

"A wife does not enjoy seeing a man monopolize her husband. In certain ways it's almost worse than having him become involved with another woman. Another woman is easier to understand, and, perhaps, to deal with. Now, if the wife happens to be attracted to the husband's friend the situation can become complicated, even dangerous."

"Dangerous," said Faith.

Jane nodded. "Yes, if the wife and the husband's friend become romantically involved. This is not an unlikely occurrence owing to the wife's almost inevitable curiosity about her husband's friend, even if at first she doesn't like this man, or pretends not to like him. It's quite common for the wife to attempt to convince herself that he disgusts her in some way. That is part of her denial of her husband's need for the companionship offered by this man."

The waiter brought their sandwiches and drinks, momentarily interrupting Jane's lecture. She sat back straight in her chair until he'd set the plates and glasses on the table and walked away, then she continued.

"If the wife and the friend do have an affair it will end badly, perhaps violently, depending on the persons involved, of course."

This is almost better than a novel, thought Faith. The woman has more depth to her than I'd imagined. "Of course," Faith said, leaning forward in order to study Jane's face more closely, "but why are you telling me this? Does it have something to do with Billy Boy's murder?"

Jane put up her right hand. "Just a moment, please," she said. "I don't want to get ahead of myself."

Faith sat back. Jane smiled briefly, then turned it off just as suddenly. Neither of the women had eaten a bite or taken a sip.

"It doesn't necessarily work the other way around, however," said Jane. "I mean if a husband becomes involved with a friend of his wife's, a woman friend. That is usually an entirely different situation, one we needn't go into here."

Faith made a mental note to ask Jane about those possibilities some other time.

"Now," Jane said, "there are exceptions. But this is not one of them."

"This?" asked Faith.

"Billy Boy wasn't murdered," Jane said. "He had himself killed."

Faith was not sure what to say. She drank some water. "What do you mean?" she asked. "How do you know this? Even if he 'had himself killed,' as you say, someone still murdered him. And why choose me to tell?"

Jane stood up. "I thought you'd understand. You're— you and Woolly—supposed to be the bright ones around here. I'm sorry, I've got to go." She walked out of the restaurant.

Faith stared at the untouched food on the plates in front of her. The waiter came over.

"Is there anything I can do?" he asked.

Faith started to laugh, then suddenly stopped. She could not recall the last time she'd been so thoroughly confused.

"No," she said. "Oh, wait. Yes, you could bring me a bag to put these sandwiches in, please. And the check. I guess this lunch is on me."

18.

MOSS WAS SITTING IN HIS KITCHEN HAVING A COFFEE and puzzling over Billy Boy's relationship with the

Down-and-Out Boys gang. He didn't think it had to do with drugs, although he couldn't be certain of that. Billy Boy's charter business was down, of course, because of his drinking; but everybody's business was down. Moss found it difficult to believe Billy Boy would have been so desperate as to hook up in dope trafficking with the Maoris. Then there were Billy Boy's apparent conflicts with Curly and that wharf rat Jeff to consider; not to mention any trouble he was having with Jane. The disappearance of the gun Moss had given Jane bothered him, too. It was an unfortunate coincidence, if that's what it was, that Billy Boy had been shot with a .38 caliber bullet.

The telephone rang and Moss answered it.

"Hello, Moss. Woolly here."

"What's up, mate?"

"Listen, the missus just told me a pretty strange story about a conversation she had at lunch today with Jane Reynolds. I think you should come over and hear it for yourself."

"All right," said Moss. "I'll be there in just a bit."

Ten minutes later Moss was sitting in Woolly and Faith's front room listening to Faith's version of Jane's narrative. When she'd finished, Faith sat back and waited for Moss to respond. When after a minute or so he still hadn't said anything, Woolly prodded him.

"What do you think, man? What did she mean about Billy Boy having himself killed?"

"Jane's not much of a liar," Moss said. "But I don't know what to think now. She told me she'd misplaced or lost something I gave her, and she's never lost track of two things in her life; she's just not that way."

"Do you think she's told this to the police?" Faith asked.

"No," said Moss. "I doubt that. I suppose I'll have to go see her and find out what's going on. It sounds to me like she's attempting to cover up for somebody."

Woolly was running his hand over and over through his beard. "Maybe she's covering up for Billy Boy," he said.

Moss looked at him, then nodded. "Stranger things have happened."

19.

WHEN HE WAS TEN YEARS OLD IN AUCKLAND, MOSS HAD seen the movie *Blackboard Jungle,* a 1955 film about what were in those days referred to as juvenile delinquents in a New York City high school. His favorite scene in the movie had been when the Puerto Rican kid, played by Rafael Campos, got up in the classroom to deliver an oral presentation of his daily routine. Campos couldn't do it without saying "stinkin' " about every other word. Of course Moss and all the other kids in the cinema knew that what Campos was really saying was "fuckin' " —"I get up in the stinkin' mornin' an' put on my stinkin' shoes, brush my stinkin' teeth and my stinkin' hair and go to the stinkin' school." Moss remembered laughing so hard during this scene that he pissed himself.

The gang kids in *Blackboard Jungle* weren't anything like the DO-Boys in Whangarei, Moss thought. He couldn't figure out what was happening now with the Maoris. They had a fair representation in the government, everything was accessible to them. It wasn't like the blacks in America or even the Aborigines in Australia. The blacks had been brought to America as slaves and the Abos were still in the Stone Age. The Maoris had come to New Zealand from Polynesia and displaced the native inhabitants, and that not very long before the *pakehas* arrived. And the Maoris had a rich history, a strong sense of tradition, unlike the whites who were largely the descendants of criminals expelled from England. Now the Maoris had formed these racketeering gangs and demanded "their" lands back. Moss could not recall a single instance of Billy Boy's making anti-*pakeha* or pro-Maori or separatist remarks prior to the night he was killed. He didn't believe that this Maori stuff had anything to do with Billy Boy's death.

20.

MOSS HAD A CHARTER WITH THREE JAPANESE businessmen. All these guys really wanted to do was to get out on the water and catch any kind of fish at all. They weren't after trophies, just a satisfying day on the water, which made them ideal customers for Moss, who specialized in kingfish and snapper. Moss ran them out to the Cavallis, close to where the *Rainbow Warrior,* the Greenpeace ship, had been scuttled. It made for good structure, and seldom had Moss failed to find fish there on a calm day like this one.

The *Rainbow Warrior* had been blown up in Auckland harbor just prior to its setting out to protest the French government's nuclear testing in the South

Pacific. Only one person was on board at the time, a photographer who, following the first explosion, went below deck in an attempt to rescue some of his equipment. He was killed by the second explosion. A man and a woman, members of the French antiterrorist force, had infiltrated the Greenpeace organization and planted the bombs. Both were apprehended by the New Zealand police, who released them to the French authorities after the French government agreed to imprison them. Each spent a brief period in detention on the French-owned South Pacific island of Hao, the man less time than the woman due to an illness, for treatment of which he was sent back to France.

The woman, Dominique Prieur, was released by then French Prime Minister Jacques Chirac just prior to the 1988 election, in an attempt by Chirac to gain support in his campaign for president against the incumbent, François Mitterand. The reasons given for Prieur's premature repatriation were that her father, who lived in France, was ill, and that she was pregnant, Prieur having been allowed conjugal visits with her husband during her detention. Prieur returned to Paris to a hero's welcome, orchestrated by Chirac's advisers, a week before the election, which Mitterand won by a large margin. Chirac immediately resigned from his office as prime minister, as he had promised he would do if defeated. Dominique Prieur and her cohort, of course, much to the displeasure of the New Zealand government and the supporters of Greenpeace, were free.

Moss Hawks did not consider himself much of a political animal. He was a fishing guide, and he stayed out of the world's business; but even he could not help but be outraged by the callous activities of the French government. The French occupation of their South Pacific territories galled Moss, especially that recent nasty business in New Caledonia. They should get out of it, Moss thought. Civil wars, tribal disputes, Moss reckoned, were one thing; interference by a third party was quite another.

He thought about this while he guided the Japanese tourists around the Cavallis. It was an extraordinarily beautiful spot. Moss had spent almost five months on one of the more remote islands during his tenure for the Parks and Maritime Commission; not only did he know the area well, but he was quite attached to the place. Some of the islands had a few goats on them, but most were totally uninhabited and covered by a variety of subtropical vegetation. He hadn't minded the *Rainbow Warrior* being scuttled out there, but the thoughts its presence conjured up in his mind—nuclear devices, duplicitous governments, murder—disturbed him because they were so out of place. This was an area in which he'd always felt free of the world's agonies, and his own. The realization that there was no place left on earth that remained untainted by man's unsavory behavior tempered the pleasure and solace he took in the beauty and seeming isolation, an intrusion Moss deeply resented.

The Japanese businessmen caught several yellowtail apiece, along with a couple of scorpion fish and a half-dozen *kahawai,* and one of them brought up a large moray eel, which Moss sliced off the line. The angler who'd hooked the eel protested, saying the eel would have made good eating. Moss didn't discuss the matter with him, just tied on a new leader and lure and told him to put his line back in the water. A large mako slid under the boat, exciting the Japanese, who tossed their lines after it; but Moss explained to them that the shark would not go for the lures designed to catch kingfish. The shark, Moss said, had been attracted by the burley, or chum, the fish particles Moss chopped up and released into the water around the boat. It bothered Moss that his mind was occupied by thoughts other than those having to do with fishing. This was not the way he wanted things to be.

21.

THE CONNECTION BETWEEN BILLY BOY AND THE DO-Boys bothered Moss, and he decided to check into it further. He went over to Whangarei on the *Yellowtail Two,* tied up at the dock, and walked to the pub. It was about four-thirty in the afternoon, a neutral hour, Moss figured. He thought this might be the best time to talk to Mister Mongrel about Billy Boy.

Moss didn't know what to expect; he was prepared to be ignored, but he didn't expect any of the gang to pull a violent stunt with him. Several DO-Boys were at the bar and two others were at a table toward the back. Moss went over to the bar and ordered a Rheineck. The Maori bartender didn't even look at Moss, just gave him his beer and took his money.

"I'm looking for Mister Mongrel," Moss said to the

DO-Boy leaning on the bar nearest him. "Is he anywhere about?"

The DO-Boy didn't look at Moss, either, but he pointed his thumb back over his left shoulder toward the table occupied by the two gang members.

"Thanks, mate," Moss said, and walked to the rear of the barroom.

"My name is Moss Hawks," he said to the larger of the two Maoris. "Are you Mister Mongrel?"

"That's me," said the DO-Boy leader.

"Billy Boy Reynolds was a mate of mine," said Moss. "I understand you knew him."

"I know many people. Billy Boy is one of them."

"You know he's been murdered?"

"I know people alive and I know them dead. Either way, I still know them."

"I was hoping you might be able to tell me something that would help me find out what happened to Billy Boy," Moss said.

Mister Mongrel and his buddy both laughed.

"You already know what happened," Mister Mongrel said. "Billy Boy is killed. Not much to talk about it."

Moss looked over at the bar. The DO-Boys were leaning with their backs against it, staring at him. He turned back to Mister Mongrel.

"Look, I'm not a cop," Moss said. "Billy Boy was my mate and I'd like to know why he was killed, not necessarily who shot him."

"What makes you think he didn't shoot himself?"

"There was no weapon found at the scene and no powder burns on his hands," said Moss.

"Why would you think I'd know anything?" said the DO-Boy. "And what makes you think I'd tell you if I did know? Besides, you *pakehas* know we blacks don't have very good memories. Tomorrow nobody will care about if Billy Boy is alive or dead. He is only one less Maori, you see? What is one Maori alive or dead in the world?"

"Forget I troubled you then," said Moss.

"Oh, it's no trouble to forget, mate," said Mister Mongrel. "You see, you live long enough you forget, too. You forget Billy Boy, you forget why you come here, you forget you come here at all. It's better that you forget. If you need help forgetting, you come back another time soon and see me. I can make you to forget, no trouble."

Moss walked out of the bar without saying anything else. As he was crossing the bay he thought about the first time he had fished with Billy Boy. Moss did not have his own boat yet and they had gone out on Billy Boy's launch, the *Trouble Ahead*. That boat was long gone, but the legacy of its name lived on in Billy Boy's wake.

22.

MOSS ANSWERED THE TELEPHONE ON THE THIRD OR fourth ring, he wasn't sure. It wasn't quite morning yet, the sky was still dark, and he'd intended sleeping in since he didn't have a charter that day.

"Moss, you awake?" It was Woolly Larrabee.

"Am now, mate, thanks to you. What's up?"

"Coppers arrested Mister Mongrel and another DO-Boy for Billy Boy's murder. They're in the lock-up at Whangarei."

"Where'd you get this bit?"

"Hunt Terry heard it from Dannie Martin, a skipper from Opua who was in the pub in Whangarei when the inspectors took 'em away. Had to do with drug traffickin', they say. Billy Boy'd been transportin' weed

down from Whangaroa for the DO-Boys to supplement his income and run into some disagreement on
the split."

"Makes sense," said Moss.

"Does, unfortunately. Didn't mean to disturb your
kip."

"Thanks, Woolly."

Moss hung up and stared into the blackness. Roxanne snored lightly next to him. Billy Boy had been a
decent enough fella, Moss thought, but like most creatures in or out of the water, once he took the bait he
couldn't spit out the hook.

Man don'

        tell me

  that no

          real

   woman

  anyway

    I take

      her

The Bearded Lady
of Rutgers Street
‰‰‰‰‰‰‰‰‰‰
New York

MANY YEARS AGO I WENT WITH MY FRIEND MISS BEVERLY
to have breakfast at the Garden Cafeteria on the Lower
East Side of Manhattan in New York City. The Garden
was a hangout for Jewish writers such as I. B. Singer, and
was one of the last establishments of its kind dating back
to the time when the neighborhood was populated pri-
marily by Jewish immigrants from Europe and Russia.
Miss Beverly was an uptown girl, the Upper East Side,
to be exact; in those days it was not her habit to be
caught dead, as she might have put it, below Thirty-
fourth Street, and even then only to go to Macy's at
Christmastime.

Miss Beverly was not, strictly speaking, a snob; it was just that she had her preferences. She accompanied me, as she said, to have my company on a winter morning. It was a cold day; the streets were icy, old snow was piled on the sidewalks, the sky was a dark, threatening gray. The Garden Cafeteria was a spacious, high-ceilinged place, drafty and impossible to heat sufficiently for the comfort of its customers, mainly denizens of the area, which was not one of New York's toniest. Paint peeled from the yellowed walls, and the tile floor, though regularly if not religiously mopped, bore the indelible stains of a dozen decades of traipsing galoshes and spillage of food and, undoubtedly, blood.

We stood in line and then carried our trays laden with kreplach soup and bagels with lox and cream cheese to a Formica-covered table and sat down. Miss Beverly left on her coat and hat, removing only her mittens. We ate and talked for about five minutes before a small woman, her face wrapped in a brown woolen scarf, sat down next to Miss Beverly. The woman also wore an oversized green flannel coat and a black knit hat. She removed her scarf, revealing a thin but distinct reddish-brown beard. On her tray was a large bowl of matzoh ball soup and a short stack of untoasted slices of rye bread.

Before ingesting her first spoonful of soup, the bearded lady addressed Miss Beverly.

"Do you live around here?" she asked.

Miss Beverly straightened her back, flashed a sudden deadly stare at me, then turned to the woman and said, "No. Do you?"

"Uh huh," answered her hirsute interlocutress, "right here on Rutgers Street. You eat here often?"

She pronounced the T in often emphatically.

"Not often, no," replied Miss Beverly, with a silent T. "And you?"

"Every day. They got great soup. I like matzoh balls. You?"

"I prefer kreplach."

"I don't eat meat myself," the woman informed Miss Beverly, "only with others."

She held her spoon still for a moment and stared at Miss Beverly, watching for a sign that she had gotten the joke.

"Oh?" responded MB, who then smiled.

The bearded lady emitted a brief laugh that sounded

more like a loud hiccup, then continued eating. In between spoonfuls of soup, she pushed a piece of rye bread into her mouth. It appeared to Miss Beverly, and to me, that the woman had swallowed the slice of bread without first having chewed it.

"My daughter doesn't like to come here," she said. "She doesn't like Jewish food. I love it, it's filling."

"Does your daughter live with you?" asked Miss Beverly.

"Not no more, not since she got married. Her husband's a fireman in Yonkers. She moved up there. He's Irish, like me."

"So you're not Jewish?"

"I wish I was. You?"

Miss Beverly nodded.

"Jews got it all," the woman said.

"What have they got?"

"The hatred of the whole world. The Jewish people are guilty in the eyes of all the other inhabitants of this earth."

"Guilty of what?"

"Being right. It's one thing to be right, but another thing altogether to claim it. You go around telling everyone you're the chosen people, you put a bull's-eye on your back."

The bearded lady finished her soup, saving the matzoh balls for last. She took her time with them.

"The Jews won't make the same mistake twice, though," she said, after she had disposed of the second and last matzoh ball. "Next time around, they'll keep their mouths shut so nobody can blame them for everything, the way it is now."

"The next time around?"

The woman stood up and said, "The Buddhists say we all keep coming back, only not always as human beings. If I'm real lucky, I'll return as a Jew in the desert, somewhere warm."

She wrapped her long brown scarf around her face, picked up the remaining slices of rye bread from her plate and stuffed them into one of the pockets of her green flannel coat.

"If the Jews are hated so much," said MB, "why would you want to be one?"

The bearded lady pulled the scarf away from her mouth and smiled. She had very few teeth.

"To justify my displeasure with everyone else," she said.

Miss Beverly stood up and took one of the woman's hands in her own, then asked, "Do you think the Jews will ever be forgiven?"

"Why should they want to be?" said the bearded lady, who leaned forward and gave Miss Beverly a little kiss— a kisslet, as MB later described it when telling this story to a friend—squeezed her hand and walked away.

Miss Beverly sat down and smiled at me.

"We'll come again," I said.

"Definitely," said Miss Beverly.

Don't eat

      my children

   take me

          I taste

  sweet

     in your

           mouth

My Catechism

ى كى كى كى كى كى كى كى كى كى

Chicago

IT WAS DURING THE WINTER I LATER REFERRED TO, IN deference to the poet, as Out of the Clouds Endlessly Snowing, that I was dismissed once and forever from Sunday school. Mine was not a consistent presence at St. Tim's, due to my mother's predilection for travel and preference for tropical places, but the winter after I turned eight years old, she left me for several weeks with her mother, whom I called Nanny, in Chicago. Where exactly my mother chose to spend that period of time I've never been entirely certain, although I believe she was then keeping company—my mother and father were divorced—with a gunrunner of Syrian or Lebanese descent named Johnny Cacao, whose main residence seemed to be in the Dominican Republic.

I recall receiving a soggy postcard postmarked Santo Domingo, on which my mother had written, "Big turtle bit off part of one of Johnny's toes. Other than that, doing fine. Sea green and crystal clear. Love, Mom." The picture side of the card showed a yellowish dirt street with a half-naked brown boy about my age sitting on the ground leaning against a darker brown wall. A pair of red chickens was pecking in the dust next to his bare feet. I wondered if the chickens down there went for toes the way the turtles did.

On this blizzardy Sunday morning, I walked to St. Tim's with two of the three McLaughlin brothers, Petie and Paulie, and their mother. My mother and grand-mother were Catholics but they rarely attended church; Nanny because she was most often too ill—she died before my ninth birthday—and my mother because she was so frequently away, swimming in turtle-infested seas. Petie and I were the same age, Paulie a year younger. The eldest McLaughlin brother, Frank, was in the army, stationed in Korea.

After the church service, which was the first great

theater I ever attended, and which I still rank as the best because the audience was always invited to participate by taking the wafer and the wine, symbolizing the body and the blood of Jesus Christ, Petie, Paulie and I went to catechism class. Ruled over by Sister Margaret Mary, a tall, sturdily built woman of indeterminate age—I could never figure out if she was twenty-five or fifty-five—the children sat ramrod straight in their chairs and did not speak unless invited to by her. Sister Margaret Mary wore a classic black habit, wire-rimmed spectacles, and her facial skin was as pale as one of Dracula's wives. I had recently seen the Tod Browning film, *Dracula,* featuring Bela Lugosi, and I remember thinking that it was interesting that both God and Dracula had similar taste in women.

During instruction, the class was given the standard mumbo jumbo, as my father—who was not a Catholic—called it, about how God created heaven and earth, then Adam and Eve, and so on. Kids asked how He had done this or that, and what He did next. I raised my hand and asked, "Sister, *why* did He do it?"

"Why did He do what?" she said.

"Any of this stuff."

"You wouldn't exist, or Peter or Paul, or His only son, had He not made us," answered Sister Margaret Mary.

"I know, Sister," I said, "but what for? I mean, what was in it for Him?"

Sister Margaret Mary glared at me for a long moment, and for the first and only time could I discern a trace of color in her face. She then turned her attention away from me and proceeded as if my question deserved no further response.

Before we left the church that day, I saw Sister Margaret Mary talking to Mrs. McLaughlin and looking toward me as she spoke. Mrs. McLaughlin nodded, and looked over at me, too.

The following Sunday morning, I was about to leave the house when Nanny asked me where I was going.

"To the McLaughlins'," I told her. "To Sunday School."

"Sister Margaret Mary told Mrs. McLaughlin she doesn't want you coming to her class anymore," said Nanny. "You can play in your room or watch television until Petie and Paulie come home. Besides, it's snowing again."

You can

    no

      give me

            more trouble

   than I have

     already have

This Coulda Happened Anywhere

સ્ট્રસ્ટ્રસ્ટ્રસ્ટ્રસ્ટ્ર

Buenos Aires

Aʀᴛ Aᴄᴇᴠᴇᴅᴏ ᴅɪᴅ ɴᴏᴛ ᴡᴀɴᴛ ᴛᴏ ᴛᴀᴋᴇ ᴛʜᴇ ꜰɪɢʜᴛ ᴡɪᴛʜ Fernando "Diablito" Lima in B.A., but Bug Gelb said he had no choice in the matter, not if Art wanted Tucker. So okay, he took it. Bug Gelb didn't get a sharp thrill thinking about going back to Argentina, either, he told Art, but let's go, do the thing, hop on a plane the same night.

Art lit a cigarette, his second that day, one over his limit, and sat down at the kitchen table. It was close to midnight. Flora and the kids were asleep. He heard the whistle from the 11:58 hi-ball to Watsonville. As a kid, Acevedo had trained himself to wake up to hear the whistle because it was his old man's run and Art knew his pop would be coming in the door around 12:30. Manuel Acevedo had worked for twenty-nine years as a brakeman out of the Southern Pacific yards, raised four children, and then died of a heart attack six months following his retirement. Art was thirty-six years old and he still woke up every night at two minutes to twelve.

Art had lost a bum decision to Luis Spota in Buenos Aires three years before and had vowed after that never to return. Now he had to or lose the last chance he would ever have to fight for a belt. Tucker's people were putting him through it because they could, because Tucker wanted no part of Diablito Lima, and it was either make the trip or hang 'em up. Fanucci would take his action, Art knew, if he wanted to go that way, name the round. The temptation was there, go out with a sock full. How much was the title shot worth to him, that was the question. Art took a last puff at 12:04, put out his cigarette and sat there. At 12:31, he went back to bed.

"Don't torture your brain, Art," Bug Gelb said, as the plane touched down in B.A. "Lima ain't Spota, this is three years later. Anyway, all's you got to do is put out his lights. You see the crack, *bang!,* you go through it. That's our guarantee, Bob."

Acevedo had trained hard. One easy workout down south would be enough, Bug Gelb figured. If Art could avoid the Argentine's hook off the jab and shoot the straight right in with authority, Diablito would go. That straight to the chin was their prayer, the only mother-grabbing thing Art Acevedo had remaining to him. Bug Gelb did not let go of his wedding ring until the airplane came to a complete stop. Estelle was gone now four years, after forty-eight years of marriage. She communicated to Bug Gelb through his wedding band; he heard Estelle's voice through his fingers. "Wear the blue tie with the gray jacket," she'd tell him. Or, "Don't trust that *gonif* Fanucci, he'd sell his mother's burial plot."

At the weigh-in, Fernando Lima looked perfect, not an ounce over or under his predicted weight. Art Acevedo came in three-quarters of a pound over, just under the limit. He didn't look perfect to Bug Gelb, but as Estelle's mother said out loud to her daughter after being introduced to her future son-in-law for the first time, "Looks ain't everything, darling, long as he knows how to get the *gelt.*"

Midway through the third round, Art felt his legs going. "What's wrong?" Bug Gelb asked him when he came back to his corner. "All of a sudden you're like a bumpkin in a funny mirror." "Cramps," said Acevedo. "My legs're gooey." Their cut man, Marvis Elster, started immediately to knead Art's calves.

"Keep close," Bug Gelb ordered. "Don't throw the straight right unless he backs off. Try'n nail him with an uppercut, both hands." "He can take it," said Art. "Nobody can take an uppercut," said Bug Gelb, "it lands solid. Hadn'ta been for the weight differential, Conn woulda whipped Louis with it. Stay up in there, Art, catch him once, then clobber him with the hammer he don't sink right away."

In the fourth and fifth, Art took too much punishment. He tried to crowd Diablito but the Argentine twirled, dipped, toe-danced, dug into Acevedo's sides. By the beginning of the sixth, Art had no stems whatsoever, badly bruised ribs, and had not come close to scoring an uppercut. The miracle came when the Argentine stumbled over Art's right foot and nearly took a header. Acevedo unloaded his right hand down on Lima's left ear. From the neutral corner, trying to stand on no legs, breathing like a Chinaman so as to minimize the pain from his ribs, Art Acevedo saw Diablito Lima still on the canvas, only the referee was not counting him out. Instead, the ref was kneeling next to the Argentine, talking to him. Then the referee stood up, waved his arms above his head a few times, turned toward Art and pointed at him, waved his arms again, turned back to Lima, whose handlers were now in the ring hoisting him to his feet, grabbed one of Diablito's hands and thrust it in the air. The Argentine's handlers led Lima out of the ring.

Bug Gelb and Marvis Elster accosted the ref, who kept shaking his head. By now there were many people in the ring and Art couldn't figure out what was happening. Marvis Elster appeared and shouted at Art that the referee had disqualified him for throwing a rabbit punch which had rendered Fernando Lima unable to continue, and declared the Argentine the winner. Marvis attempted to get Art moving but he could not. Bug Gelb got hold of his fighter's left arm and tried to wrap it around his shoulders but Art would not let him pry it from his side.

"Where are we?" Art asked. "We in Buenos Aires,"

said Marvis Elster, "an' been jobbed again." Bug Gelb fingered his wedding band. Estelle was berating him for having gone back to Argentina in the first place. "For Christ's sake," Bug Gelb said, "this coulda happened anywhere."

There she is

    letting

        you want

          it

    she's a saint

        don't cross her

          or you

            wake up

            with

              the devil

          sitting on

            your

              chest

One Leg

Germany

In September of 1965, when I was eighteen years old, I traveled from London, England, where I was living, to Hamburg, West Germany, with my friend Oscar Jürgen Schmidt. Oscar was twenty. We'd met at a boarding house in Chelsea I'd lived in for a few weeks after I'd first arrived in London, and where Oscar still resided. He was apprenticing at a coffee company, learning the business from an associate of his father's, who was a coffee importer in Hamburg. I was writing music and working for a publishing firm. Our holidays fell at the same time and he invited me to accompany him to his home in a small village just outside Hamburg.

We traveled by train and ferryboat. Oscar's parents welcomed me warmly. Oscar's younger brother, who was thirteen, showed me a framed photograph of John F. Kennedy hanging on a wall in his room. Ever since Kennedy had made his *"Ich bin ein Berliner"* speech he had been a heroic figure to the youth of West Germany. After his assassination, in 1963, Kennedy became something more on the order of a saint.

In Hamburg, Oscar and I visited the offices of his father's coffee company and walked around the city, which reminded me a great deal of my native Chicago. We took a boat ride on the inlet that led to the North Sea. Even though it was only September, the air was cold. I recall thinking that I did not want to be there during the winter.

One evening after dinner at the house, I asked Oscar's father about his participation in World War II. He said that he had been a major in the German army, stationed for much of his service at the Russian front. About the concentration camps and the mass extermination of the Jews by the Nazis, he said he had known nothing until it was too late. I asked him what he meant by too late and he told me that by the time he understood what was happening, the end of the war was fast approaching, the German forces were in retreat from Russia, and there was nothing to be done, at least by him. Frau Schmidt said that before the war they had advised some Jewish friends to leave the country. So you knew the worst was coming, I said. Nobody could have known how terrible it would be, she replied.

My friend Oscar, I could see, was becoming uncomfortable with the conversation, so I stopped asking questions of his parents. Later, however, I asked him if, when he was in school, the Holocaust had been discussed. No, he said. We were told only that a great many innocent people had suffered, as always happens during a war.

The next afternoon, Oscar took me to visit a neighbor, a Swiss woman who lived on a large property populated by hundreds of songbirds. She was very old and had lived on this estate, she told me, for more than sixty years. Her first husband, she said, had been the Kaiser's right hand man. He was killed in the Great War, as she called it. After him, there had been three more husbands, all of whom she had outlived. Now I have my birds to serenade me, she said. On our way back to his house, Oscar told me that her next-to-last husband had been a high-ranking official in the Nazi party. My father says it's the only reason she survived, said Oscar. What do you mean? I asked. She's a Jew, he said, not really a Swiss. Her husband protected her. I've seen photographs of her when she was young. You can't imagine, looking at her now, how unbelievably beautiful she was.

Oscar and I took a bus from Hamburg to Berlin. This meant that we had to travel through Communist East Germany, which was occupied by Russian troops. I was the only passenger on the bus who was not a German national. When we stopped at the East German check-point, the authorities made me get off the bus and questioned me as to my purpose for traveling to Berlin. I told them that I was a tourist, visiting Germany with my friend. After twenty minutes or so of discussion among themselves, the officials made me pay for a special visa, filled a page of my passport with stamps and signatures and allowed me to get back on the bus. The other passengers eyed me with suspicion. This was the height of the Cold War and everyone was paranoid. Unlike Oscar, who was upset that my presence had caused a delay, I was more amused and interested than annoyed. They only wanted money, he said, once the bus was again on its way toward Berlin. My father is angry that Germany has been divided, he continued, that a part of it is controlled by the Russians. He doesn't dislike the Jews, said Oscar, but he hates the Russians.

After exploring West Berlin, Oscar and I decided to visit the eastern part of the city. The wall forced us to enter by different routes. Being a West German citizen, Oscar had to pass through Friedrichstrasse, while I chose to walk in at Checkpoint Charlie in the American sector. We agreed to meet at a particular place in East Berlin but somehow we missed each other, so I wound up exploring the mostly rubble-strewn city by myself.

That night I went into a bar in the neighborhood where the writer Bertolt Brecht had lived. More than thirty years later, after Berlin was unified and the wall had been torn down, I had dinner in Brecht's house, which had been turned into a fancy restaurant. In 1965, however, East Berlin was a very gloomy place. In the bar, I met a one-legged man who told me that he was an ex-Legionnaire. He'd left the majority of his left leg, he said, in North Africa. I asked him why, if he was a German citizen, he had joined the French Foreign

Legion. I was living in Belgium, he told me, in Antwerp, and I had to kill a man who tried to cheat me in a diamond deal. I was completely justified in doing what I did, but I didn't want to risk a trial so I skipped to France, took the oath and got sent to the desert. I was stationed on the outskirts of Oman, and was doing well enough. Everyone in the Legion is a pervert of some kind, at least they were then, but I could take care of myself. The war came and suddenly I was in Morocco fighting against my own countrymen. I got captured and when the Germans found out I was their kind, instead of murdering me like they did the rest of our bunch, they shot my left leg full of holes, left it dangling by a thread. One leg, they told me, is all half a German deserves to have, and they stranded me in the desert.

Arabs found me, got me up on the back of an ass and took me to a British field hospital, where a doctor took off what remained of the limb. Half a German, they called me. Now we are all of us half Germans, the country split into pieces. They should have shot me to death, as they did my comrades. *Vous ne serez jamais seul,* we say in the Legion. You'll never be alone. My right leg is alone. He misses his brother. If I could get out of here and get to America, perhaps I could work in a factory. Is there a job in America for an old man with one leg?

The next morning, I crossed back into West Berlin and found Oscar walking back and forth in front of the bus station. He knew I would go there eventually. Oscar asked me where I'd spent the night. I said I'd stayed up in a bar talking to the one-legged ex-Legionnaire. On the bus back to Hamburg, I told Oscar the story the man had told me. I don't believe it, Oscar said. Did he ask you for money? No, I said. In fact, he bought me several beers. He did ask me if I wanted a girl, though. The bus was passing through a beautiful forest. Oscar, whom I would last hear from a few years later, when he was working for a coffee exporting company in Mombasa, said, Maybe he wasn't lying, after all.

We preserve
        ourselves among
    ignorant beasts
by appearing
            as angels

The Stars Above Veracruz

ഗ്രൗഗ്രൗഗ്രൗഗ്രൗഗ്രൗഗ്ര

Mexico City

I WAS SITTING AT A TABLE BY MYSELF IN LA FAENA, A cantina on calle Venustiano Carranza in the Centro Historico that used to be frequented by bullfighters. There were still toreros' costumes on display in glass cases and a sign at the entrance that said Museo de Toreros. At night bands came in and played but no bull-fighters were there to hear them. That time was gone. I still liked to go to La Faena but only when the place was virtually empty, late in the afternoon around five or six. The waiters were always polite. They were old and they looked old, as old as the costumes under glass. Sometimes tourists wandered in and stayed long

enough to inspect the costumes and have a beer or a
tequila but they rarely came again. The floor tiles were
dirty. Everything was dirty and dusty and there was no
paper of any kind in the washrooms.

Paco brought me a fresh Indio and took away my
empty. A one-legged man on crutches lurched over to
the jukebox and dropped in a few coins. Julio Jaramillo
began singing and the man lurched over to a table on
the other side of the room and eased himself into a
chair. There was a glass of tequila and a Coronita on his
table. The crippled man finished off the tequila in two
swallows then started in on the short beer. He'd probably been there for a while but I hadn't noticed him
until he fed the juke. Other than his missing leg he was
unremarkable to look at. His skin was light brown; he
was maybe forty-five or fifty years old. After Julio
Jaramillo finished *"Amor sin esperanza,"* Agustín Lara
began singing *"Revancha"* and I felt as if I knew the
one-legged guy a little bit.

I sat with one hand wrapped around my bottle of
Indio and thought about the Eurasian girl I'd left back
in San Francisco who'd told me I reminded her of a
white tiger. One day she came home with a ceramic

figurine of a white tiger she'd bought in Chinatown and showed it to me. She was so happy to have found it. It looks just like you, she said, and made a place for it on the nightstand next to her bed. For all I know it's still there. She was a beautiful girl and a very nice one, too, but she was a lush and I never could tolerate for very long a woman who drank too much. She always wore the same perfume, a fragrance of gardenias called The Stars Above Veracruz, which did not so much sweeten or adorn as seem to inhabit her skin.

I was thinking about how painstakingly the Eurasian girl tweezed her eyebrows every morning even if she were hungover when the one-legged man started shouting. I couldn't understand what he was saying because he was across the room and Agustín Lara was still singing but when he pulled a revolver out of his coat pocket I hit the deck. When in doubt, my old man used to say, get down fast and stay there until the shooting stops. It was over quickly because there was only one shot fired. Agustín Lara quit at just about the same moment the gun went off. I waited for thirty seconds or more before I looked over and saw that the crippled man had used the *pistola* on himself. One of the waiters bent down and inspected the fellow up close, and then walked away shaking his head and crossing himself. I climbed back up into my chair.

Paco came over to me holding a bottle of Cinco Estrellas and a glass. He poured the glass full and set it down on the table. On the house, señor, he said. The revolver was still clasped in the corpse's right hand, resting on his chest. I picked up the glass of rum and took a swig. I thought then that I would like to have been in bed in San Francisco with The Stars Above Veracruz in my nostrils and the Eurasian girl who called me her white tiger. She had dove-shaped hands with long slender fingers and she really loved me, she really did.

In the end
    it all
  comes down to this
      don't it
It's a losin' game
      I know
    but it's
            the only
      one
          counts

Coda: The Ropedancer's Recurring Dream

I AM IN A FOREIGN CITY ON A CHILLY, DAMP NIGHT, walking with a friend, a man. Strangely, I am wearing only boxer shorts and a T-shirt. I'm disturbed about something, angry. We are about to cross a street, which is deserted; there is very little or no traffic. I've been resting my arm on a signpost and when we move I accidentally hit the sign, which falls over. As I cross the street, I look back to see the sign lying on the sidewalk. I momentarily consider going back to pick it up, but I don't. When my friend and I get to the other side of the street, two cops approach me and ask for my identification. They are women, both wearing hats and

trenchcoats. I tell them that I don't have my passport
with me—I don't have any pockets—only some paper
money wedged under the waistband of my shorts. They
point at the fallen sign and inform me that knocking it
over is a crime. My friend, who is a resident of the city,
attempts to intervene but the cops place us both under
arrest for malicious mischief, charging me also with
lack of identification. I tell them they can come with
me to where I am staying and I will produce my passport but they insist on taking us directly to the police
station.

At the station, the female cops seem proud of themselves as I am booked. My friend, because he is a citizen, is given a citation to appear in court or choose to
pay a fine and is released. I am formally charged and
placed alone in a cell. I'm cold and wet, shivering,
furious. The cops say nothing can be done until I produce my papers. I tell them again that I've left everything at home. They've separated me from my friend,
and I ask the women to tell him to go to my place and
get my passport and whatever other documents are
required of me and bring these things to the station. He
has already gone, they tell me, it's too late. I am to be

arraigned in court. When? I ask. That depends, say the cops. I know I'm dreaming but it doesn't matter; I am in a foreign country and there is nothing I can do.

Barry Gifford

Barry Gifford's novels have been translated into twenty-seven languages. He is also the author or co-author of numerous screenplays, including *Lost Highway, Perdita Durango, City of Ghosts,* and the forthcoming *Portovero.* The film based on his novel *Wild at Heart* won the Palme d'Or at the Cannes Film Festival in 1990. Mr. Gifford's most recent books include *The Phantom Father,* named a *New York Times* Notable Book; and *Wyoming,* named a *Los Angeles Times* Novel of the Year. For more information please visit www.BarryGifford.com.